IN THE SHADOW OF THE
MOUNTAINS OF MADNESS

PIERCE MOSTYN PARANORMAL INVESTIGATIONS
BOOK 8

C W HAWES

CWH BOOKS

In memory of Joe West,
who was, perhaps, the one who started it all.

ENTER THE IMAGINATIVE WORLD OF CW HAWES

Enter my world. A world of terror on a cosmic scale. Just click, tap, or scan the QR code below.

Fear is the most primal of human emotions. And fear of the unknown is the most terrifying of all fears.

If you are new to the Pierce Mostyn Paranormal

Investigations series, then *In the Mountains of Madness* is an excellent entry point into the series and into my world.

In addition to my Pierce Mostyn Paranormal Investigations books, I've written short stories set in the world of the macabre and arcane. Many of which are only available to folks on my mailing list.

So just click, tap, or scan the QR code to enter my world of terror and the macabre. You will get a free copy of *The Feeder* and you'll get my monthly email of news and curated contact. Terror awaits!

1

VOSTOK STATION, Antarctica

The wind blew swirling eddies of snow around one of the crushed Quonset huts. Special Agent in Charge Pierce Mostyn took in the destruction of the Russian Antarctic base camp. Hell's Furies had cried, "Havoc!", and torn the place apart.

Yet this was not the destruction humans would produce. There was a curious otherworldly aspect to what had happened. There was the unidentifiable slime and the decapitations. And that triangular print in the snow that something had made. Whatever had caused this destruction, it was something Mostyn didn't want to dwell on for too long.

Next to him stood Admiral Arthur Danforth, commander of the US rescue operation. "Whatever happened here, happened fast. I don't think those poor devils knew what hit them."

Mostyn nodded. "I'd hazard a guess that whatever it was, it came up from Lake Vostok through the borehole."

"The borehole is larger than normal. Am I correct?"

"You are."

"Which means something dug its way *up* through the ice."

"That's my guess."

"What the hell could do that?"

"Beats me, Admiral. What we do know is there are no polar bears here, so we can't blame them."

"Killer penguins?"

To himself, Mostyn said, *If only you knew the truth.* Out loud, he said, "You could try running with that story."

The admiral let out a laugh. "Maybe. For now, I'm keeping the messages cryptic. The less said the better."

"Good idea."

"Your photographer is having a field day."

Mostyn nodded. "Although I think he'd rather be photographing penguins. The normal kind."

"You're probably right about that. God, those poor devils."

Mostyn excused himself and walked over to one of the few huts that was still standing. It had been a field hospital. Now it was a morgue.

He opened the door and entered, moving from 5° F to 65° F. He closed the door and walked to where forensic anthropologist Doctor Dotty Kemper was bent over one of the deceased, examining the body.

"Anything you can tell me, Dot?"

Without taking her eyes off of what she was examining, she said, "This one appears to have been dissected. While alive."

"Good Lord."

Dotty's head turned towards Mostyn, and her eyes caught his. "He isn't too good if he allowed this to happen."

"What else can you tell me?"

She turned back to her work. "The others were butchered like cattle."

"Were they...?" Mostyn let the question hang.

"Used for food? I don't know. All the bodies are missing parts. Some organs. Some limbs. Death came quickly for most."

"I'll leave you to your work."

Dotty stood up and turned to face Mostyn. "We're not here on a rescue mission, are we?"

"No."

"It's those damn mountains, isn't it?"

Mostyn nodded.

"I knew it." She shook her head and turned back to her work. "I remember him talking about them. The Mountains of Madness. I'm surprised he didn't come with us."

Mostyn smiled. Dotty Kemper remembered everything. Forgot nothing. The incident took place four years ago and had been in actuality a brief side conversation. A simple reminiscence by Doctor Rafe Bardon of his time in Antarctica.

"He is older, you know," Mostyn said. "But who knows? He might surprise us and show up."

"That's all we need. The boss watching everything we do."

Mostyn chuckled. "Catch you later."

He left the hut. His eyes took in the horizon. *God, it's cold,* he thought. Even with the sun shining and the temperature near zero, the windchill made the air feel like it was fifteen degrees below zero. The blinding glare coming off the snow rendered the tinted goggles less than adequate, forcing Mostyn to put his hand up to shield his eyes.

He noticed Admiral Danforth's engineer was with the three scientists who were part of his team.

For this assignment, Mostyn and his people were passing themselves off as a group of scientists supposedly operating under the auspices of the National Geographic Society. In actuality, he and his team were operatives of the ultra-secret US Office of Unidentified Phenomena. An agency so dark, that fewer than three dozen people in all the federal government were even aware of its existence. The president wasn't on the need to know list.

Mostyn made his way over to where the scientists and engineer were examining the borehole. The equipment was a wreck, and the hole was mostly closed up, but traces of where it had obviously been enlarged were visible.

The geologist, Doctor Daniel Smithson, was discussing the puzzling problem with the others as Mostyn joined the group.

Smithson pointed to the ridge circling around the borehole. "That is clear evidence something came *up* through the ice, probably from the lake, and was large enough that it needed a four, four and a half foot diameter channel."

"That's a good sized creature," Doctor Terri Lynn Dyer, the team's marine zoologist said.

Landon James, the engineer with Danforth's rescue party, was shaking his head. "How is that even possible? From everything I've read, we're talking microbes in that lake. Perhaps some form of unicellular protozoa. Not a monster that's three or four feet wide."

Doctor Wilfred Heidegger, the marine biologist assigned to Mostyn, shrugged. "It is difficult to dispute what we see." His accent betrayed him as a native of Germany.

"Nope. Not buying it," James said. "There has to be another explanation. One that's normal, natural."

"How do you account for the deaths, the destruction, and those odd triangular-shaped prints we found?" Mostyn asked.

James shrugged. "Somebody went crazy. Killed everyone and wrecked the place."

"Perhaps," Mostyn said. "Perhaps."

And as far as the outside world was concerned, Mostyn thought, *that would most likely be the story they would hear.*

Doctor Bardon, however, suspected otherwise — and that's why Mostyn and his team were there at the bottom of the world.

2

Washington, DC — Eight Days Earlier

Pierce Mostyn sat in the office of Doctor Rafe Bardon, director of the Office of Unidentified Phenomena, or OUP as it was usually referred to when it was referred to at all.

Bardon's office was decorated in a style suitable for a nineteenth century British men's club. Mostyn was in a dark chocolate brown leather tub chair facing Bardon's massive black walnut desk. The little round Englishman was seated behind the desk and busily lighting his pipe. When he had it going and a cloud of sweet Virginia pipe tobacco was on its way to the ceiling, Bardon spoke.

"You read much Lovecraft?"

"No, sir. Robert E. Howard is more to my liking."

Bardon smiled. "Ah, Pierce, my boy, Howard does suit you. The man of action. Even so, did you ever read Lovecraft's *At the Mountains of Madness*?"

"A long time ago. I'm afraid I found it frightfully boring, if I remember correctly."

Bardon chuckled. "Do you remember any of the story?"

"Not really, sir."

"That's actually very good. You won't be prejudiced." Bardon evaded the questioning look on Mostyn's face. "There's an interesting backstory to Lovecraft's novel. One that is not generally known."

"The novel's based on fact?"

"In a measure. The book was heavily fictionalized for the pulp magazine market. There was in fact a Doctor William Dyer, and he did lead an expedition to Antarctica in 1930. Lovecraft corresponded with Dyer. Unfortunately, the letters are lost. We're aware of the correspondence because Lovecraft mentioned it to several of his correspondents."

"How much of Lovecraft's book is fiction?"

"That, too, we aren't sure about. The mountain ranges and the city as mentioned by Lovecraft are fiction. However, the Gamburtsev Mountains, which are a subglacial range, are just about spot on where Lovecraft quotes Dyer as giving the location of the Mountains of Madness. And the sub-glacial lake Lovecraft mentions, could correspond with Lake Vostok or another, as yet undiscovered, lake."

"Apparently, you think Dyer found something in the area around the Gamburtsev Mountains."

"Let's just say I know he did, and unfortunately I can't say anymore."

Mostyn nodded, and thought, *Typical dark op think*. To Bardon, he said, "So why are you telling me this?"

Bardon chuckled, "Cut to the chase, eh, my boy? The reason I'm telling you all this is because I have a mission for you."

"In Antarctica?"

"Precisely."

"But nobody lives there. At least permanently."

"No *humans* live there permanently. Lovecraft was not writing fiction when he wrote about the coming of the Elder Things from somewhere deep in space and of their residing on the mega-continent Rodinia after their initial sojourn in the ocean." Bardon leaned back in his chair and puffed on his pipe before continuing.

"The Russians are in trouble. Underneath their Vostok station, lies Lake Vostok. By volume, it is the sixth largest lake in the world, and because it is a freshwater lake, we could say it is the sixth Great Lake.

"The Russians, out of nationalistic pride, were hellbent on drilling through the ice and into the lake to discover if life is there. This was important to them because that lake is one of the last unexplored regions on the earth. Reaching the lake, in their opinion, would make up for losing the space race to you Americans. The Russians were first in space, first to send a man in orbit, first to reach the moon. They won all the battles, but lost the war when the US landed men on the moon. It's all about pride."

Bardon puffed on his pipe, sending a thin stream of sweet smelling Virginia tobacco smoke drifting towards the ceiling. He then resumed his narrative.

"Well, they succeeded. They drilled into the lake two years ago. However, in their haste, they didn't take proper precautions. The first freshwater sample they brought up was heavily contaminated with boring fluids. Supposedly they have taken a pristine sample." Bardon shrugged. "But they are Russians. And Russians say a lot of things."

"I take it, you think this has caused a problem."

"Ah, Pierce, my boy, right on the money. Three weeks ago, Vostok went silent. The Russians attempted a rescue mission, but their plane crashed in a storm. After diddling around for another week, they finally asked Washington for help, and the government agreed. A week from now you'll be at Vostok station. You and your people will be attached to the US rescue mission. When your work is done there, you will receive instructions for a second mission."

"A second mission, sir?"

"For now, let me say you and your team will push on to the Gamburtsev sub-glacial range. The true Mountains of Madness."

"But if these mountains are below the surface of the ice sheet, how did the Dyer expedition find them?"

"A very good question, and I'm afraid I can't answer it. Lovecraft had Dyer teaching at Miskatonic. In actuality, he was a professor at another small school, which filed for bankruptcy in the eighties. For whatever reason, the FBI never added Dyer's papers to their X-Files. Which is most unfortunate, as Doctor Dyer's notes, photographs, and drawings have largely disappeared. The few papers we have do not provide an answer."

"Let me see if I understand correctly what you've said.

Something happened to the Russian base. You believe it may be connected to their drilling into this sub-glacial lake and polluting it. And because we know the Elder Things were originally marine creatures and probably returned to the sea when Antarctica froze over, you feel there's a connection here between Lake Vostok, these sub-glacial mountains, Dyer's expedition, and now this problem with the Russians."

Bardon sat up and was all smiles. "Excellent! Well, done, Pierce."

A faint smile touched Mostyn's lips. He'd just gotten a gold star from his boss. Mostyn took in a deep breath and exhaled. "When do I leave?"

"Tomorrow morning. Your team will assemble at the McMurdo Station and join the US rescue mission, and you will all fly from McMurdo to Vostok."

Bardon slid a thumb drive across his desk, and Mostyn retrieved it. "Background for you and instructions for the first part of your mission." Bardon puffed on his pipe, then said, "I believe this is your month with Helene."

How does he know that? Mostyn said to himself.

"She'll be going with you, as well as Doctor Kemper. I'm assuming there will be bodies, and I want Doctor Kemper's expertise. She and Helene have been getting along?"

"Yes, sir, they have."

"Good, good." Bardon stood, and Mostyn did as well. "Good luck to you, Pierce."

"Thank you, sir."

They shook hands, and Mostyn left.

On his way to his car, he pondered his new mission. Antarctica. He sighed and shook his head. If he remembered correctly, Lovecraft had written that the Elder Things had ultimately been destroyed. Which meant he and his people might be dealing not with those ancient beings, but their slaves. The ones who destroyed them. The shoggoths.

3

VOSTOK STATION, Antartica - The Present

Admiral Danforth caught Mostyn just as he was about to enter the mess hut. "Mind if we talk a minute?"

Mostyn told Helene and Dotty to go on in and save him a seat. "What can I do for you, Admiral?"

Danforth pulled Mostyn around the corner of the hut. "I've been watching your people... "

"Any particular reason why?"

"Other than Heidegger, Dyer, and Smithson, your people don't strike me as civilian types. You aren't, are you?"

"I'm not sure I understand what you're getting at, Admiral."

"Sure you do, Mostyn. What are you guys? CIA? Defense Intelligence?"

"We're a bunch of civilians working under the auspices

of the National Geographic Society. If you don't believe me, check with the society."

Danforth smiled. "Right. I've had experience with you black ops types before."

"Okay. Let's say we are. Is that a problem?"

"No. I just want to know who I'm working with. That's all."

Mostyn smiled. "However, if we were black ops, I don't think we'd be telling you. Would we?"

Danforth laughed. "No. I don't suppose you would. Although you just did." He held his hands up. "Just so long as it's the Russkies you're checking out, I don't care what you do."

The smile was still on Mostyn's face. "I can't tell you what to believe, Admiral, but we are just civilians."

"Okay, Mostyn. Whatever you say. Enjoy your dinner."

The admiral departed and Mostyn was left wondering what the hell that was all about. He shook his head and entered the hut. The cook was standing behind a table with two open cardboard boxes on it.

"Step right up and take your pick of the finest dining the US military has to offer." The cook pointed to the first box, then the other. "Take your pick. The price is right. A lifetime of gastrointestinal problems."

Mostyn chuckled and looked at what was left in the boxes. He rooted around until he found a Menu #1 packet. Chili with beans. He told the cook thanks, and made his way over to the table where Helene, Dotty, Baker, Jones, and NicAskill were seated. Jones saw him and waved.

"Hey, Boss, got a seat for ya," Jones called out.

Mostyn took the seat. He didn't know how Jones did it, but no matter where they were, or what they'd been through, the special agent always managed to look like a Greek god.

Sitting next to him was Kymbra NicAskill. She could look like a hard-ass combat veteran, or a very attractive woman looking for a night on the town.

"What kept you?" Baker asked.

Mostyn had known Willie Lee Baker, along with Dotty Kemper, from when he'd first joined the OUP. Baker was a world-class photographer and got pudgier and pudgier with each passing year. It didn't bother him. Mostyn was amazed at how comfortable Baker was with himself. There were days he wished Baker could give him a bottle of whatever it was he had.

"The admiral wanted to talk," Mostyn said in answer to Baker's question.

"Anything in particular?" Dotty asked.

"I'll fill you in later," Mostyn answered. "Find out anything of value?"

Jones nodded and in a hushed voice said, "I think two of the alpine rescue workers are CIA. Brown and Wood."

"I think we can add the radio guy," NicAskill said.

"When were you talking with him?" Jones asked.

"He came to me. Even gave me his phone number."

Jones just grunted and shook his head.

"I'd put LuAnn Getz, the nurse, in that group. She was hanging around and kept asking if I needed help," Dotty said.

"I don't have anything to add on that score," Baker said,

"but I can say that whatever it was that went through this base was efficient and knew what it was doing."

"Any guesses based on past experience?" Mostyn asked.

In hushed tones, Baker answered, "Whatever it was, it wasn't human."

Two images appeared in their minds. One was of a creature that was part animal and part plant. The thing had wings, a star-shaped head, and a star-shaped pseudo-foot. Instead of arms and hands, it had tentacles. The second image made Dotty gasp and shudder. It was the image of a rubbery protoplasmic spheroid, a viscous agglutination of a bubbling froth of cells, infinitely plastic and ductile. It was the image of a shoggoth.

Helene said verbally, "Those were the beings that were here."

"How do you know this?" NicAskill asked.

"When my people came to this planet with the Great Old Ones, there was a war with the Elder Things and their slaves. I have not seen these beings. But they figure in our literature, our histories, and our art. Those headless bodies—"

"Covered in frozen slime," Dotty interjected.

"Yes, my sister. Those were killed by the shoggoth. The others by the Elder Things."

"Holy shit," Jones said. "There's just no getting away from these monsters."

Helene smiled. "No, DC. This continent is the home of the Elder Things. It is their sacred land."

Jones buried his face in his hand and groaned.

Baker chuckled. "Welcome to the OUP, Jones."

"Why is this such a surprise?" Dotty said. "It's not like you joined yesterday."

NicAskill put her hand on his shoulder. "I think our boy here is tired of fighting monsters. He'd like a normal job and a house in the suburbs with a white picket fence."

Jones looked at NicAskill. "And what's wrong with that?"

NicAskill touched his nose with her forefinger. "Nothing, Jonesy."

"Is there something you two aren't telling us?" Mostyn asked.

They looked at each other and then at Mostyn. In unison, they said, "No, Boss."

"Yeah, right," Mostyn replied. "And my uncle is the president."

Helene had a puzzled look on her face. "He is?"

Everyone burst out laughing.

4

THE SUN WAS JUST a few degrees above the horizon. Mostyn had watched it move around the horizon all day. How different that was from the way it moved back home.

After supper, he'd had the team gather in one of the unused Russian huts. That particular hut was not off limits. No one had died in it, and it showed no signs anyone or anything had entered it either during or after the attack.

Mostyn looked at the nine people standing before him. His team. "We're going to make this meeting quick. I don't want to arouse any suspicion that we aren't who we say we are. Although people may already suspect we are intelligence agents. Admiral Danforth has voiced his suspicion to me."

"What do you mean?" Agent Parker Jackson, the team's drone expert, said.

"Before supper, he pulled me aside and straight out asked if we were CIA or Defense Intelligence."

"Are we that obvious?" Jones asked.

"To him, at least," Mostyn replied.

"Is this a problem for us, Mostyn Pierce?" Helene asked.

"Not really. Unless someone makes it a problem. I think the admiral was just curious. After all, this is a Russian base. It only stands to reason we'd include operatives from the intelligence community in the rescue mission. Even the Russians know that. Which is probably why it took them a week to ask for our help."

"So what are we to do, Boss?" Jones asked.

"Collect all the data you can. With the radio operator being most likely CIA, send only the most mundane information through him. Sensitive intel goes through our own equipment."

"We understand, or should I say we surmise, that the perpetrators of the attack were not human," Doctor Heidegger said. "I assume we keep this information to ourselves."

"Very much so," Mostyn said. "We must keep the true nature of the perpetrators a secret. Our mission is to find out why they attacked. Any further questions?" Mostyn surveyed the group and when he saw no one had any questions, he dismissed everyone except for Jones, Dotty, and Helene.

"Dotty, is there a way to secure the bodies?"

"Do you mean lock them up?"

Mostyn nodded.

"No."

"As I thought. Jones, I want you to set up a watch to stop anyone from getting too nosey."

"On it, Boss." Jones made his way out into the Antarctic night.

"Helene, I want you to dematerialize and see if you can find out what the admiral suspects about us and to find out who's in charge of the CIA operatives."

"Yes, Mostyn Pierce. Should I go now?"

"Yes."

Helene vanished.

"Dotty, make sure your notes are encrypted."

"Always," she replied.

"Good. And get them back to Bardon ASAP."

"Will do."

He and Dotty stood outside the hut, holding gloved hands, and looking at the low hanging sun.

"I'm surprised about DC," Dotty said.

"He's in love."

She laughed. "Is he ever." After a pause, she said, "I'd like a house with a white picket fence."

"You would?"

"Yes, I would. I'm getting sick and tired of hunting monsters for Bardon. And if I'd known we'd be running into a goddamn shoggoth, I'd have told him to count me out. Once was enough for me, thank you very much."

"So you don't think the family that fights shoggoths together, stays together?"

"Don't go into comedy, Mostyn. You won't make it."

"I'll keep that in mind, Kemper." He paused for a moment before continuing. "Tell Bardon you want a desk job. For now, though, we're here at the bottom of the world. We have a job to do."

Kemper sighed. "All right, Mostyn. For Bardon and country. Let's kick some shoggoth butt."

Mostyn smiled. "That's my girl." He took Dotty Kemper in his arms and whispered, "I love you, Dot. Perhaps we should start looking for that house."

Dotty leaned in to kiss him, and a scream ripped through the night air.

5

A SECOND SCREAM WAS CUTOFF. Mostyn pushed off the hood of his parka so he could better hear where the commotion was coming from. When he got what he thought was the location, he pointed, and he and Dotty Kemper began running.

They rounded the corner of one of the Russian buildings and there in the midnight sun was a massive sphere, a blasphemous black agglutination of protoplasmic bubbles. A shoggoth. Scores of eyes appeared and disappeared over the entire surface of the thing, and there was the constant high-pitched utterance of *"Tekeli-li! Tekeli-li!"*

The horror began changing shape, forming itself into a dome over the field hospital, turned morgue.

"What the hell does that thing want with a bunch of dead bodies?" Kemper asked.

"Don't know, Dot, but we have to destroy it."

Someone ran up to the monstrosity and opened fire with a pistol. The shoggoth extended a protoplasmic "arm" and covered the person. A moment later the pseudo-arm withdrew and a headless, slime-covered body stood for a moment, as if turned into a statue, before it collapsed to the snow and ice.

Jones appeared, hurled an object at it, and hit the ice while yelling, "Cover!"

Mostyn and Kemper hit the snow-packed ice moments before the blast of the grenade ripped through the night air.

He looked up and watched what remained of the shoggoth slowly begin to dissolve, as if it was being eaten by a powerful acid.

Emitting a screech almost beyond human hearing, the thing divided. Half continued to dissolve, while the other half began rolling towards Jones.

From the other side of the blasphemous monstrosity, NicAskill yelled, "Cover!" A small can bounced and rolled in front of the horrific nightmare. There was a pop and a sheet of flame.

The shoggoth emitted a high-pitched, flute-like sound, before it was completely incinerated by the intense heat and fire of the thermite grenade.

Mostyn and Kemper got up and walked over to the morgue. They watched as the last bits of the evil entity dissolved. The prefab metal walls of the building were scorched. Slime covered the ice and snow surrounding the hut, and where the snow and ice had melted in the grenade blasts, the water was refreezing.

In front of the building was another body. Headless and slime-covered.

Jones and NicAskill joined Mostyn and Kemper. A crowd was forming, and Admiral Danforth had to push his way through to reach Mostyn.

"What the hell was that thing?" Danforth asked. "It looked like something out of a B-grade horror movie."

"Don't know," Mostyn said.

"Like hell you don't," Danforth replied. "Your people knew how to deal with it. And what the hell are you doing with grenades here, anyway? Now I know you aren't a bunch of goddamn civilians. What are you? Special ops?"

Mostyn looked at Danforth. "Can't tell you. You don't have clearance."

"I'm TS/SCI approved and have Yankee White."

"Sorry, Admiral. I doubt God could get clearance for what I and my people do."

"Shit. So I'm just supposed to sit in the dark while some movie prop murders my people?"

"As of this moment, I am assuming command. Code Delta, Echo, Alpha, Delta, Eight, Romeo, Whiskey, Juliet."

"What the hell, Mostyn?"

Special Agent in Charge Pierce Mostyn ignored the admiral and turned to a man standing next to him. "You're the radio operator. Moore, is that right?"

"That's me," Moore replied.

"When did we last get a weather report?"

"About six hours ago. A storm is moving in our direction. Should be here by noon tomorrow."

"Tell McMurdo we need an immediate evac. The rescue team needs to leave before the storm hits."

Danforth was furious. "Belay that order, Moore." The

admiral turned to Mostyn. "You wait one minute. I don't know who you think you are—"

"I'm the guy who's going to save your bacon," Mostyn replied. "You have no idea what you're dealing with here."

"That may be, but my team is going nowhere. It's staying right here."

Mostyn turned from the admiral to the radio operator. "Send the message, Moore. The admiral has been relieved of the command of this mission. I'm in charge now, and the longer we argue about this, the greater the danger we're in."

Moore looked from Mostyn to Danforth and back to Mostyn. "By whose authority are you in charge? You spouted off a bunch of letters and numbers, but what do they mean?"

The admiral's second in command, Major Felix Tipton, pushed his way through the cluster of rescue mission personnel and stood next to his boss. "What's going on, sir?"

Before Danforth could answer, Mostyn said, "I've relieved the admiral of the command of this mission. I've assumed command, and I'm sending you all home."

"By what authority?" Tipton asked.

Mostyn repeated the code.

Tipton looked at Danforth. "That's Homeland. And it means this site is—"

"I know what it means, Tipton," Danforth said. "The fucking little green men code." The admiral turned his back on Mostyn, then turned to Moore, and said, "Send the goddamn message," before storming off to his hut.

To all the people who'd been listening to the exchange, Mostyn said, "Everyone under Admiral Danforth's command prepare to leave. Your part in this mission is over."

The group began to break up. To his own people, Mostyn said, "I want all of you to keep an eye on our equipment. We can rest assured that there are plenty of intelligence agents in this group and I don't want them accidentally on purpose taking anything that doesn't belong to them. Jones, you coordinate. Dotty, you're to make sure the morgue is secure. Dismissed."

As the team members were leaving, Helene Dubreuil walked up to Mostyn. "Do you feel it, my husband? The evil? This is not a good place."

"And, unfortunately, where we're going isn't going to be any better."

6

THE EASTERLY WINDS howled and buffeted the Quonset hut. Admiral Danforth's team had taken off in a giant military cargo plane mere minutes before the storm swept down upon the base. The only one who was thrilled with the raging winds and blinding snow was Helene.

"I never experienced anything like this in K'n-yan. All of these new experiences!"

She insisted on going for a walk in the storm, and Mostyn finally relented but made sure that a rope was tied around her waist so she could make her way back.

"That woman is crazy," Dotty declared.

Jones, with a smirk on his face, said, "How can you say that about your sister?"

"Shut up, Jones," Dotty shot back. "And she's not my sister."

Peals of laughter came from Jones, and it was difficult for some of the others to suppress the sniggers and smiles.

"How can you all laugh like that? Don't you feel that, that...?" NicAskill began.

Helene reappeared out of thin air, with no rope around her waist, and interjected, "That evil."

"Geez, you scared me," NicAskill said, hand upon her chest.

"I am very sorry. Please forgive me."

NicAskill shook her head. "No problem. Don't worry about it." She took a deep breath. "I wasn't going to put it that way, *evil*, but, yeah, I suppose you could call it that."

"It's a kind of dis-ease," Baker said.

"Gives me the heebie-jeebies," Doctor Terri Lynn Dyer confessed.

Mostyn, to change the subject, asked, "Are you, by chance, related to the late Doctor William Dyer?"

"Yes," she replied. "He was a great-great uncle, or something like that."

"Did you know him at all? Did he tell you anything about his Antarctic expedition? Or speak of it to anyone in your family?"

"Not really. And I was pretty young when he passed. I do know he didn't want to talk about it, to anyone, and when he finally did talk, it was to try and stop that follow-up expedition. But everyone thought he was crazy, and didn't listen to him."

"The expedition was canceled, however."

"Yes, but that was due more to a donor backing out than anything my uncle said."

Mostyn nodded and thought on that for a few moments

before asking, "So there's no family lore, no stories about the expedition?"

She shook her head. "Like I said, he tried to warn people and stop that follow-up mission. Otherwise, as far as I know, he kept everything to himself."

"The wind is coming from the mountains, and it is scented with the ancient evil that is there," Helene said.

"How can that be?" the geologist Smithson said. "I assume you're talking about the Gamburtsev Mountains, or the Ghost Mountains."

"The Mountains of Madness my uncle called them," Dyer said.

Smithson chuckled, "This is just wind." When Baker started to say something, Smithson held up his hand. "Yes, yes. The things that go bump in the night. Bardon's my boss, too, remember. No offense, Doctor Dyer, but your uncle and his team were a group of polar amateurs. I think this place just got to them."

"In other words," Dyer said, "you believe they all went crazy."

"Probably not all, but at least one and probably more of them did."

"What about the shoggoth?" Baker said. "I think just about everyone saw it. Maybe what Lovecraft wrote was basically true. Maybe, Smithson, there *is* a city, and a vast subterranean sea, and loads of shoggoths."

"Don't go overboard, Willie Lee," Dotty cautioned.

"They are here," Helene said. "The creatures that created you. That created humans."

Everyone looked at Helene. But before anyone could ask

what she meant, Mostyn said, "All we know, at this point, is that we have a print that could be the footprint of an Elder Thing, that Vostok Station was attacked and destroyed, with no survivors, and that we were attacked by a shoggoth."

"That's a hell of a lot right there, Boss," Jones said.

"Seems to me," NicAskill added, "we're in the thick of it."

"Right where Bardon wants us," Dotty said.

"I must tell you," Doctor Heidegger began, "I feel this undefined fear, this anxiety, or nervousness, too. It is palpable. What is the saying you Americans have?"

"You can cut it with a knife?" Baker suggested.

Heidegger nodded. "Yes, that is it, Mr. Baker."

"Just remember," Mostyn said, "this is a mission no different from any other."

"When things are going bump in the night, who ya gonna call?" Jones said.

"The OUP!" NicAskill and Baker said in unison.

Dotty rolled her eyes, "Oh, for the love of God."

A vicious gust of wind shook the hut, and something banged the side of the building. Dyer let out a scream.

"Want me to check it out, Boss?" Jones asked.

Mostyn shook his head. "Something probably blew loose in the wind and hit the building on its way to who knows where."

"I do not think so, Mostyn Pierce," Helene said, and disappeared.

Mostyn sent his thoughts to her and ordered her to return to the hut.

"One of these days she's going to get in trouble doing that," Dotty said.

Helene reappeared. "We have visitors, Mostyn Pierce. The Elder Things have returned."

And intermingled with the howling of the wind was a peculiar piping over a wide range.

7

JONES SAID, "I say let Ms. Stealth dematerialize us, NicAskill and myself, and we hit them."

Mostyn inhaled a lungful of air and slowly exhaled. "We don't know how many of these things we're dealing with."

"What difference does it make, Mostyn?" Dotty argued. "Jones is right on this. We need to get rid of as many of these things as we can."

"I know this isn't a democracy," Baker said, "but I'm with Jones on this one."

Doctor Heidegger added, "If they see we can bite, and bite very hard, then maybe they will leave us alone."

"Or we piss them off," Doctor Dyer said.

"Headquarters has a supply plane on its way," Mostyn said. "When it gets here, we'll have reinforcements and more tools to deal with these things."

"So we leave them out there?" Jones said.

"For now, I think that's best," Mostyn replied.

"Where's Helene?" Dotty asked.

Mostyn looked at the floor and shook his head.

"She was here a minute ago," Doctor Smithson said.

"Is anything missing?" Mostyn asked.

Helene reappeared. "This is so exciting!" In Helene's hands was a strange-looking object.

Jones said, "Nope. Nothing missing."

"What on earth were you doing?" Mostyn asked, his volume just shy of yelling.

"Saving us," Helene replied. "Such a new experience. This tool works very well. You should have seen how they just flew apart. Even the shoggoth."

"There was a shoggoth out there?" Dotty asked.

"Oh yes, my sister. There were three Elder Things and a shoggoth. They are very much fascinated with the hospital. Two of them were in the building with the shoggoth. I went inside the building, reappeared, used this tool to disintegrate the shoggoth, and disappeared. The Elder Things were so surprised they almost fell over each other trying to get out of the building."

"So the disruptor worked without a problem?" NicAskill asked.

"Why didn't you just make them disappear like you always do?" Jones asked.

"It is difficult to dematerialize a shoggoth. They are very loosely made and are always changing. But this...," Helene looked at NicAskill.

"Disruptor. M101 E."

"Yes, this disruptor," Helene said, "catches everything, and it just disintegrates. It is very exciting! A new experience!"

"New experience aside," Mostyn said, "I didn't give you permission to act."

"You are not happy, Mostyn Pierce?"

"They may be angry and send more."

"I don't think so." Helene had a big smile on her face. "I dematerialized one of the destroyed huts and rematerialized it in the borehole. They cannot reach us that way. At least for now."

"Way to go, Helene!" Jones said.

There was a general murmur of approval. Even Dotty Kemper was smiling.

The look on Mostyn's face was a clear admission of defeat. "What about the Elder Things?" he asked.

"I used this tool to disintegrate them as well." She set the weapon down and clapped her hands like a child. "It was so fun, Mostyn Pierce! I followed the two from the hospital and let them get to the hole in the ice and then shot each one. I even let the third one get into the hole before I disintegrated it. If only my people had these."

"Thank God they don't," Kemper said.

On hearing Dotty's words, Helene's excitement vanished. Her tone now sober, she said, "Yes, you are right, my sister. I would not be here, and neither would you, nor DC, Mostyn Pierce, or Willie Lee."

"You have that right," Baker said.

"I am sorry," Helene said. "I forget myself."

"Don't worry about it," Mostyn said. "We're all here and it seems you've bought us some time. There are no more out there?"

Helene shook her head.

"Good job. Although next time I'd like you to talk to us. There's no room for loose cannons on this team."

"What is a 'loose cannon'?"

"I'll tell you later," Dotty said.

To the group, Mostyn said, "The immediate threat is over, and this phase of our mission is complete. Now I have to inform you about Phase Two."

"I knew it," Jones said. "Nothing's ever simple with Bardon."

"Ah, quit griping, Jones," Baker said. "With the hazard pay you can buy a nice house in the suburbs and get a desk job to spend more time with the kids."

Mostyn had to look at the floor as he failed to suppress the smile on his face. For the first time, Jones was speechless, and beet red.

"What is the next phase of our mission?" Doctor Dyer asked.

Mostyn lifted his head. "We are to go to the Mountains of Madness and locate the city of the Elder Things."

"And let's hope that goddamn disruptor doesn't crap out on us," Dotty said.

8

MOSTYN WATCHED the giant military cargo plane disappear over the horizon. They were alone. Deep in the Antarctic interior. Nothing but ice and snow as far as the eye could see. At the moment, because Helene had blocked the Russian bore hole to Lake Vostok, there was no danger from unwanted visitors bent on doing them harm. Yet for all that, Mostyn still felt a palpable dis-ease, an uneasiness that made its way under the skin and stayed there.

He turned around and looked to the east. Out there, lying some two thousand feet under the ice, were the peaks of the Gamburtsev Mountains. The Mountains of Madness. Beyond them lay the Vostok Subglacial Highlands. Is that where the sacred city of the Elder Things would be found? Mostyn let out a wry chuckle. Would they find anything at all? Maybe Doctor Dyer had sold Lovecraft a boatload of hooey.

His gaze turned to the pile of equipment and supplies. Jones and Kemper were bringing the new people Bardon had sent up to speed. He would address everyone later and provide details of the mission's next phase, which would include the use of the strange machines sitting on the ice and snow.

Doctor Bardon had gone all out to make sure the next phase of the mission would be a success. Aside from the equipment, he'd sent three Special Forces personnel, and all three had trained in the arctic and been on missions in Siberia. They'd encountered shoggoths on previous missions and knew what to do should the team encounter more of the horrific monstrosities.

Furthermore, one of the Special Forces team, Amber Bailey, had visited, in her dreams, the terrible plain of Leng and the mysterious land of Kadath. She was also a collector of the strange and disturbing paintings of the Russian mystic known as Nicholas Roerich. The other two, JoEllen Tamsworth and Alexander (Sandy) Schwartz, while they hadn't been on any dream-quests, they had, according to Bardon, adequately demonstrated a sensitivity to mystical forces.

The OUP director had also sent an archeologist, Doctor Julia Pridmore, who would be able to analyze any ruins they might come across. She'd studied the crumbling remains of the most ancient cities and written acclaimed monographs on the similarities that tied together many ancient civilizations.

Finally, there was the OUP's engineer extraordinaire, Doctor Fritz Obermann, and his assistant Carl Wulfe. The two strange machines sitting on the ice were Obermann's invention: the Vanesco Ice Borer. Although the machine didn't so much bore its way through the ice as melt its way.

What Mostyn didn't like was that the machines were still in the experimental stage. This expedition was to be their initial test run.

All we need is for these things to break down a mile under the ice, Mostyn thought. *We'd be the new Operation Deep Freeze.*

Bardon had yet to send instructions. Mostyn thought they'd have come with the new team members; however, Bailey had told him when they arrived that all they knew was that they were to join Mostyn and his team.

He let out a sigh and walked over to the Vanescos. They were essentially a cylinder mounted on caterpillar tracks. There was a conical drilling apparatus on the front, and fins radiating from the body of the cylinder. There were windows in front and a door in the side, as well as a hatch in the top and one in the bottom.

Mostyn chuckled to himself. The machines reminded him of the Iron Mole from the movie *At the Earth's Core*.

"Do you like my machine, Mr. Mostyn?"

Mostyn extracted himself from under the machine to see a man's face peering out of a hood at him. The man extended his hand, Mostyn took it, and the man helped him to his feet.

"You're Doctor Obermann, I presume," Mostyn said.

"You presume correctly, young man."

They shook hands as Jones, Kemper, and the other new arrivals joined them. Mostyn greeted his new team members and got names to go with the faces that he didn't know.

"I'm going to find Baker," Jones said, "so we can get the food organized for lunch."

"Have at it," Mostyn told him. Jones left, and Mostyn addressed Kemper. "Why don't you show the new folks around and introduce them to the others."

"Sure, Mostyn." Dotty led everyone off to the cluster of pallets where the rest of the team was at work unpacking the equipment and supplies.

Taking a last look at the Vanesco, Mostyn set off for the radio. He needed those final instructions from Bardon. That he didn't have them by now indicated to Mostyn there was a problem.

9

THUS FAR, one hour into the morning, the Vanesco Ice Borers had worked like a charm. The only "problem" Mostyn could see at the moment was that they were slow. A top speed of only thirty miles per hour. Which meant they had about a fourteen hour trip from Vostok to the subglacial mountains.

Hydrogen fuel cells ran electric motors that powered the machines. The hydrogen came from either bottles of compressed gas, or from water broken down by electrolysis.

Doctor Obermann was driving the lead machine, and his assistant Carl Wulfe was driving the second machine. To get water for the fuel cells, the borers had melted into the ice up to the midpoint of the cylindrical bodies and were now melting a trench six feet deep by six feet wide across Antarctica. The melt water providing the hydrogen for the fuel cells.

Mostyn was in front with Obermann, ostensibly as copilot of the machine, although he had little idea how the thing actually worked. He looked out the window at the passing icescape, even though his eyes were just above ground level.

He'd made contact with Bardon the day before, who'd apologized concerning his tardiness in sending instructions for the next phase of the mission.

"Bureaucracy, my boy, bureaucracy," Bardon had said.

Apparently someone had said something to somebody who'd told yet another person of strange goings on with the rescue mission to Vostok. Usually these things tended to peter out and go nowhere. Usually. In this case, the final person in the chain was a big shot with the defense contractor that handled the staffing at McMurdo. He'd apparently talked to his boss, who talked to a certain congresswoman of his acquaintance, who'd started, once more, trying to find out who knew what about a certain Office of Unidentified Phenomena.

When asked what the upshot of the whole thing was, Bardon had chuckled, and said, "There's a bit of amnesia going about around here." Mostyn had smiled at Bardon's solution. The little round Englishman did enjoy ancient esoteric Egyptian magic. Although there were times that Mostyn thought there was nothing Egyptian about Bardon's ancient magic.

As for the second phase of Mostyn's mission, it was simple. Bore down through the ice until they located one of the mountain caves mentioned in Lovecraft's narrative, then enter the cave, get to the city, and see what they could see.

"That's all you want us to do?" Mostyn had replied. "Just look around?"

"Well, if you happen to come across an Elder Thing or two, do try to capture the beings. Will you?"

Mostyn assured his boss he'd do his best to capture an alien entity. However, Mostyn was also pretty sure there was more to this mission than Bardon was telling him. Sure, capturing an Elder Thing would be akin to proving God exists. But Bardon wouldn't have sent a team to Antarctica just on the off chance they'd find an alien being, let alone get the chance to capture one. Bardon suspected something else was going on, and that's why Mostyn found himself en route to the Gamburtsev Mountains. The Mountains of Madness.

It's for me and my team to find out if there is a danger, and if there is to stop it, he said to himself.

———

The ice boring machines came to a stop at quarter to seven. Even though technically evening, the sun was still relatively high in the sky, and being summer would not set at all. The Sat Navs on the machines told them they were directly above the mountain range. Mostyn gave the order to exit the vehicles and set up camp.

Four tents were pitched in the lee of the big borers to provide some shelter from the wind. Obermann and Wulfe opted to sleep in the machines. For supper, Baker fired up the little cook stove to heat the military MRE's, brew a pot of coffee, and make hot chocolate for the non-coffee drinkers.

After everyone had eaten, Mostyn held a meeting.

"This part of our mission is mostly undefined," he began. "We are to penetrate the ice, melting and drilling our way down to the mountains. We are then to find a cave and enter in the hopes of finding a branch or tunnel that will take us to ground level."

"Did Doctor Bardon tell you what we are looking for?" Doctor Julia Pridmore asked.

"No," Mostyn replied, and then amplified. "I'm convinced he thinks there is something here, but he won't say what. When that happens, as team leader, I have to make the ultimate call regarding anything we do find."

"In other words," Doctor Dotty Kemper said, "we're either wasting our time and taxpayers's money, or this is a mission that could see us all get killed."

"What's the matter, Kemper," Jones said, "you tired of the same old, same old? This is how it always is."

"Well, I'm tired of it," she shot back.

"There may be nothing here," Mostyn said, "and then again this may in fact be a fabulous archeological find. And as far as I recall, these creatures don't breathe ice, just air, or water. So I don't expect to meet up with any."

"So why are *we* here?" Amber Bailey asked.

"You're like travel insurance," Mostyn said. "You probably won't be needed, but if you are…"

The look on Bailey's face said she didn't believe him. "We sure have a hell of a lot of firepower for nothing," she replied.

"Better safe than sorry," Mostyn said. "Now, if there are no more questions, or comments, let's get some sleep. We have a long day ahead of us tomorrow."

Everyone made their way to their tent. Mostyn, though, remained standing, looking down at the ice between his feet.

Those shoggoths and Elder Things had to have come from somewhere, he thought. And he wasn't convinced Lake Vostok was the only place where they'd taken refuge.

So where have they been for the past thirty-five million years? he asked himself. It was a question he wasn't sure he actually wanted answered.

10

THE BORERS MELTED and drilled their way into the ice. Moving back and forth in a zigzag pattern, they crawled deeper and deeper into the Antarctic ice sheet. Nothing but white was visible through the windows.

The electricity produced by the motors drove the tractor treads and generated heat, which radiated from the bodies of the machines through the fins that covered the outer surface. The heat melted the ice and turned much of the water into steam, which fell back as snow and ice crystals when cooled by the Antarctic air.

Mostyn watched the gauge, which recorded their descent. Three hours had gone by and they were only eight hundred feet below the surface of the ice sheet. At their current rate of descent, they'd need another eight to ten hours to reach the highest peaks.

After taking another look out the window, he turned to Doctor Obermann. "When do you think we'll encounter the mountains?"

"Difficult to say, Mr. Mostyn. We are, for all practical purposes, flying blind, as they say."

Mostyn took in a deep breath and slowly exhaled. He looked at the depth gauge and the hologram map, based on soundings and guess work. He guessed they'd need to go another two thousand feet at least before they'd reach the surface of the mountains. And then would they be able to travel on the land? Would the surface be smooth enough?

He shut his eyes. No sense worrying. They'd find out when they got there.

Mostyn's eyes flew open. There'd been a jolt, and the Vanesco was sitting at an odd angle.

"You fell asleep," Doctor Obermann said. "Just as well, though, that you're awake. I believe we've reached land."

"We have?" Mostyn shook his head to clear the sleep induced fog. "How long have I been asleep?"

"Nearly seven hours."

"You're kidding me."

Obermann shook his head.

"Man, I must've been tired. Now what?"

"We're still in the ice, and have most likely reached an exceptionally tall peak, or the ice sheet isn't as thick as was previously thought. We'll keep boring and see if we come across one of Doctor. Bardon's caves."

Obermann picked up a microphone and flipped a switch. "Doctor Obermann here. Hold on tight and make sure your seatbelts are fastened. We might be in for a rough ride."

He flipped a couple of switches and began speaking.

"Vanesco One to Vanesco Two. This is Obermann. Are you there? Wulfe, are you there?"

"I'm here, Doctor Obermann."

"Very good. Now that we've encountered the mountains, we will continue our descent."

"Yes, sir."

"Follow my lead. Obermann out."

Mostyn watched Obermann fiddle with a few of the controls, and then the Vanesco lurched forward. The ride was indeed bumpy as the machine slowly crawled over the rocks, depressions, and outcroppings. The drill mounted on the front of the machine helped smooth the path somewhat, otherwise Mostyn didn't think they would have made it.

Hour after hour the two machines crawled along the side of the mountain in a switchback pattern, descending deeper and deeper into the Antarctic ice sheet.

The depth gauge read two thousand eight hundred and seventeen feet below the ice field surface when everything in front of them crumbled and fell away before the massive drill, revealing nothing but impenetrable darkness.

Obermann stopped the machine and flipped a switch. Powerful lights came on, brilliant lamps, which, along with the running lights, failed to penetrate the Stygian blackness beyond twenty or thirty feet.

"Where are we?" Mostyn asked.

"A very good question, Mr. Mostyn. I'd say we've broken into some manner of bubble, as it were. A pocket in the ice. Shall we proceed?"

"By all means. Let's see if we can determine how large this bubble is."

Obermann started the machine moving again. He continued driving in the switchback pattern as the machine crawled down the mountainside.

Not much was visible in the bright lights illuminating the darkness. Frozen rock and soil. That was it. To Mostyn's eye, everything looked as though it had been smoothed over. He mentioned his observation to Obermann, who told him that was most likely due to the action of the glaciers as Antartica got colder and froze.

They'd crawled another eighty feet down the mountainside when the first cave opening appeared. Mostyn ordered Obermann to stop and announced that they were going to explore the cave. Sixteen men and women piled out of the two vehicles dressed in hooded parkas, thermal underwear, and insulated outerwear. Mostyn had them assemble in front of the cave mouth.

"We have found a cave. If in his story, Lovecraft accurately recorded what Doctor Dyer told him, that is, in other words, Lovecraft didn't just make up the entire story, then these mountains should be honeycombed with tunnels that will eventually bring us to the great sacred city of the Elder Things. What we might encounter or what we will see is not known. Which is why we are heavily armed. The entrance is wide enough, so we will enter in pairs. Jones and I will go in first; if the passage is clear, I'll radio back for you all to follow. Questions?"

Seeing none, Mostyn turned and entered the cave with Jones at his side.

11

MOSTYN TOOK IN THE WALLS, floor, and ceiling of the cave. The stone was black with tiny spots that reflected back the light of his and Jones's lamps. Hundreds, thousands of little stars winking on and winking out as the lights passed over them.

Jones touched the wall. "Looks like most caves I've seen."

"It does," Mostyn said, and pushed on, moving deeper into the dark tunnel.

To Mostyn's eye, nothing appeared to be manmade. Nothing but water, and maybe wind, working on the stone until the whole thing became imprisoned in the ice. Perhaps at one time a wet cave, it was now very dry in the cold antarctic air.

The floor remained level for about fifty feet before it started angling downwards.

"Now we're getting somewhere," Jones quipped.

"Perhaps."

They continued on for another fifty feet or so, when Mostyn indicated they should stop.

"Look at this, Jones." Mostyn pointed to the wall. "This definitely looks as though the stone has been worked."

"Yeah. The floor feels smoother, too. I'd say we're onto something."

"And I'd say you're right."

Mostyn radioed back to the team and told them to join him and Jones. In a few moments, NicAskill and Special Forces operative JoEllen Tamsworth appeared, followed by the others.

"Most interesting," Smithson said. "This cave appears to be sedimentary rock, at least mostly. Which would indicate no volcanism in the formation of the Gamburtsevs."

"Is that important?" Mostyn asked.

With a smile, Smithson said, "To a geologist, yes, to you, probably not."

Mostyn nodded. To the team, he said, "At this point it looks as though the stone has been worked. Smoothed, mostly. We probably won't find anything, but keep your eyes peeled. You just never know."

Baker took pictures to record the difference in the texture of the cave walls, while Dyer and Heidegger examined the stone for any indications of fossils being present.

"Say, Boss," Jones began, "you think we should send a drone up ahead to see if anything is waiting for us?"

"Sure," Mostyn replied. "Good idea."

Parker Jackson, the drone specialist, took off his backpack, opened it, took out a drone the size of a golf ball, and set it on the cave floor. From a pocket on the pack, he pulled out a small tablet. In a moment, the drone took off down the tunnel. Jackson projected a holographic display of the drone's camera feed so the team could see what was awaiting them.

"That's a pretty powerful light on that thing," Jones said.

"It is," Jackson replied. "Unfortunately, it cuts down the flying time."

The drone revealed nothing but empty cave tunnel that appeared to wind its way deeper into the mountain.

"I have to bring it back," Jackson said. "At least we know there's nothing there for the next three miles."

Mostyn nodded.

The drone stopped, turned a complete circle, and started back when the holographic display collapsed and the tablet went dark.

"What just happened?" Mostyn asked.

Jackson shrugged. "I don't know. The drone just disappeared."

"What do you mean?" Mostyn asked.

"Just that," Jackson replied. "One moment it was there, and the next, it's gone."

Mostyn didn't like the sound of that. He'd been with the OUP long enough to know things don't just disappear. There is cause and there is effect. Something made that little drone vanish, and Mostyn was pretty certain it probably wasn't something you'd invite home to meet mom and share a meal.

He turned to his team. "All right everyone, listen up. There may be company up ahead. Be alert. This is a case where you shoot first and ask questions later. Let's move out."

Mostyn and Jones took the lead. Bringing up the rear were Tamsworth and NicAskill. The remaining team members were in six pairs following Mostyn and Jones.

The walls of the cave were devoid of any artwork. They were simply smoothed stone. Mostyn vaguely remembered that in Lovecraft's story Doctor William Dyer had reported that the walls of the city dwellings were covered in murals. If that was true, then the Elder Things may have only decorated their dwellings. Which meant this cave was not a dwelling. So what was it for? Or did something other than the Elder Things dwell here? If that was the case, what manner of hideous monstrosity would it be? Mostyn decided he probably didn't want to know.

A mile down the cave, an opening appeared on the left. Mostyn flashed his light around the opening, which was about nine feet high and about four feet wide. He pointed his wrist light to illuminate what lay beyond the opening.

"It's a room," he said to his team members. "Looks empty."

"Just a single room?" Doctor Julia Pridmore asked.

Mostyn stepped inside the opening, shone the light around, and stepped back out. "Just a room," he answered.

They continued on, moving deeper into the cave, and progressing ever closer to ground level. The incline of the cave floor was definite, but not steep.

After an hour of walking they reached the place where the drone had vanished. Along the way, they'd passed by a couple dozen of the small chambers. All of which were empty.

"Search this area," Mostyn said. "I want to find that drone, if it's here."

The team spread out, using head lamps, wrist lamps, and handheld flashlights to examine the walls and floor.

Mostyn was kneeling, slowly panning the wrist lamp over the floor, when a scream ripped through the air. He looked up just in time to see a black shape detach itself from the wall and envelope Parker Jackson. Mixed with the scream was the heart-sinking, high-pitched piping of *Tekeli-li! Tekeli-li!*

"It's a goddamn shoggoth," Mostyn muttered, pulling out his phone, desperately trying to activate the xenophage defense app.

Someone yelled, "Get out of the way! I got this!"

Mostyn looked up and saw JoEllen Tamsworth point an odd double-barreled contraption in the direction of the creature. He watched two streams of liquid hit the bubbling, amorphous nightmare. There was a sizzling sound followed by an explosion. Protoplasm coated the tunnel and most of the team members.

"Great," Dotty Kemper spat out. "Covered in goddamn shoggoth shit."

Mostyn called out, "Tamsworth, what was that?"

"It's what Jeffries calls his shoggoth killer," she replied. "It's chlorine trifluoride and water. The chlorine compound is highly corrosive and reacts violently when in contact with water to produce poisonous gas."

Mostyn raised his eyebrows. "Poison gas?"

"It's the violent reaction that does the trick. The gas dissipates."

"Pretty clever of Jeffries," Mostyn said. "Why doesn't the water freeze?"

"Battery-powered heater."

"It's about time R and D came up with something," Jones said. "I'm getting kind of tired not having enough firepower."

"Let's keep going," Mostyn said. "And keep your eyes open. The shoggoths are getting more intelligent and crafty. Jones, take us on down the tunnel."

"Sure thing, Boss."

The team moved out, following Jones.

Puzzled as to why the xenophage hadn't activated, Mostyn examined his phone. It seemed to be in fine working order. And then he saw the no service notification.

He shook his head. *Of all the idiotic setups,* he muttered. *A defense app that requires the phone to be online.*

He stuffed the useless gadget into his pocket, took a last look at the place where Jackson had died, and with a determined look on his face, resumed the journey down the cave.

12

THE CAVE TERMINATED in a large room that Doctor Smithson told the team had probably been carved out of a chamber in the original cave. Four other tunnel entrances dotted the roughly circular wall. Mostyn noted that the ceiling appeared to be domed.

"Let's take five," he said, "before moving on."

Bailey set up a small heater, and several of the team members clustered around it. Several more took out energy bars to eat.

Doctor Pridmore walked around the chamber, paying special attention to the other tunnels coming into it. "The angle of entrance of the tunnels would match a five-pointed star," she said.

Doctor Dyer added, "Which matches a common Elder Thing motif."

"That it does," agreed Pridmore.

Smithson took a piece of chalk out of a pouch on his belt and chalked a large white triangle on each side of the tunnel entrance they'd come through. When done, he said, "This will quickly let us know which tunnel got us here. Just in case we're in a hurry."

No one needed an explanation as to why they might find themselves in a hurry. The lack of Jackson's presence was ample explanation.

Helene dematerialized.

"What's Ms. Stealth up to?" Jones asked.

Mostyn shrugged. "She doesn't tell me where she's going, and she sure as hell doesn't ask my permission."

"Helene is not a team player," NicAskill said, "that much is obvious."

"She is when it counts," Jones replied.

"Are you dissing our favorite K'n-yanian?" Baker said.

"*Your* favorite K'n-yanian," Dotty Kemper corrected.

Jones chuckled. "I sure don't envy you, Boss."

Mostyn gave him a sideways glance. "People in glass houses shouldn't throw stones."

A puzzled look settled on Jones's face.

NicAskill punched his shoulder. "He's talking about me. Us."

"Oh. But—"

Baker cut him off. "Best to take the strategic retreat here, Jones."

The Special Agent shook his head, and Mostyn informed his team the break was over. Mentally, he reached out with his thoughts to Helene and asked her to return. In a moment she rematerialized in front of Mostyn.

"Here I am, Mostyn Pierce. That tunnel," she pointed at the one she meant, "does not descend. I followed it until you called me back and it stayed level. Four tunnels branched off. I did not go down those tunnels."

"Good," Mostyn replied, "although you should let us know where you're going."

"I will, Mostyn Pierce. It is just that this is so exciting I forget. There is no ice or snow or cold in K'n-yan."

He smiled at her, then turned to the team. "Schwartz, Tamsworth, you two take that tunnel and see where it goes. Go in a thousand paces, and report."

The two Special Forces operatives entered the tunnel. Mostyn turned to Jones and NicAskill. "You two take that tunnel. No more than a thousand paces in, then report."

"On it, Boss," Jones replied.

Mostyn continued. "Bailey, you and Helene take the remaining tunnel. And, Helene?"

"Yes, Mostyn Pierce?"

"Listen to Bailey."

"I will."

"Same as the others," Mostyn said. "Go in a thousand paces and then report."

"Yes, sir," Bailey replied, and entered the tunnel, Helene following.

Mostyn took in the rest of his team. "Doctor Ober-mann, I'd like you and Mr. Wulfe to go back and bring the Vanescos the rest of the way down the mountain."

"Do you think it wise to take both machines?" Dotty asked. "I mean, it might be advantageous to have one where we came in. You know, just in case we don't make it to the bottom of this pile of rock."

Mostyn nodded. "Good point, Dot." He turned to Obermann. "You and Wulfe take one machine down to the bottom. Any problem that you can think of leaving one machine behind?"

Obermann shook his head. "No. Shouldn't be a problem."

"Okay, good," Mostyn replied. "Leave now and keep me updated."

The inventor and his assistant left.

"What do the rest of us do?" Pridmore asked.

Mostyn held up his hand. "Go ahead, Jones. Key open channel so we all hear."

"Just did, Boss. Nicky and I are a thousand paces down the tunnel. It took a curve, and we came across a doorway to a room like those we saw coming down here. Only this one has a window looking out over what I assume would be the valley. Too damn dark to see anything, though. You want us to continue?"

"Hold tight until the others respond."

"Will do, Boss. Out."

On the heel of Jones's report came that of Amber Bailey. "This tunnel looks like it might get us where we want to go. It's a series of descending switchbacks."

"Okay, Bailey, hold tight."

"Will do, sir."

Mostyn waited for the last team to report in. The time began to number in minutes, when Schwartz at last reported.

"What took you so long?" Mostyn asked.

"We went a little further than what you said," Schwartz began, "but we thought it important, and found an apartment complex here. We've counted five multi-room units and there are probably at least a couple dozen more."

"Are they all on one level?" Mostyn asked.

"These are. But it looks like there might be more levels below the one we're in. There's a broad ramp that descends."

Mostyn turned to Smithson. "Use your chalk and mark that tunnel 'Apartments', that one 'Descending', and that one…"

Mostyn keyed his radio. "Jones, does your tunnel descend or remain level?"

"At this point, it seems to remain level. We explored a bit further and just came across more rooms with a view."

"You and NicAskill return." Mostyn called out to Smithson, who was chalking the word *Apartments,* "Mark the remaining tunnels 'level'." He keyed the radio mic and told Schwartz and Tamsworth to return.

Mostyn thought a moment, then told Kemper and Baker to take the team and meet up with Bailey and Helene. He'd wait for the others and join them ASAP.

Dotty, Baker, and the scientists left, leaving Mostyn alone in the chamber.

When was the last time anything was here? he wondered, while his eyes and lamp swept over the walls and ceiling. "Except for that damn shoggoth," he murmured.

He checked his tablet. Prior to forty-five and a half million years ago, carbon dioxide levels were in the thousands of parts per million. Yet in spite of all that carbon in the atmosphere, Antarctica began icing, and continued to ice as carbon dioxide levels fell. With the Eocene-Oligocene extinction event about thirty-four million years ago, icing accelerated due to a fall in atmospheric carbon dioxide to below six hundred parts per million.

"By that time," Mostyn mused, "the Elder Things must've realized their time on land was over and returned to the sea. But now that carbon dioxide levels are at four hundred parts per million and rising, what happens when we pass the six hundred parts per million tipping point going in the other direction? Will we have not only a new crop of giant mammals to face, but these goddamn Elder Things and their shoggoths? And what if the Elder Things were in fact killed off by their slaves? Could we be in the process of unleashing the shoggoth apocalypse?"

13

THE TUNNEL WOUND its way down the inside of the mountain and exited onto what the geologist, Smithson, guessed was a plateau or a plain. There was no light coming from anywhere except the team's headlamps, wrist lamps, and flashlights, and they didn't illuminate much.

"It's pitch black," Doctor Dyer said. "How are we going to find anything? We can see, what, about twenty feet? Might as well be in a bathyscaphe looking for R'lyeh."

"And if we've already run into one shoggoth," NicAskill said, "there could be plenty more out there where we can't see them. I don't like this, Boss. Not one bit."

"I understand," Mostyn said. He keyed his transmitter and asked Doctor Obermann to report.

"I'm here, Mr. Mostyn. We're making progress, but it's not like we're on the freeway. The navigator has locked onto your signal. The estimate is another hour before we reach you. Although, I'm guessing more like two or three."

Mostyn signed off and turned to Jones. "Set up two

beacons so Obermann and Wulfe can also get a visual on us."

Jones set up the beacon lamps which flashed alternating red, white, and green light.

"Let's take a break," Mostyn said. "Probably best if you get something to eat while you're at it." He turned to Baker. "Do you have the stove with you?"

Baker smiled. "Always. I'll set it up and get some coffee and hot cocoa going."

Mostyn gave Baker a thumbs up.

While Baker fired up the little stove, the team members sat in a large circle, a portable lamp in the middle, along with Bailey's small heater, and took out MRE packets. After the usual round of trading, everyone ate their meal, mostly in silence. When the hot beverages were ready, Baker filled cups.

Mostyn didn't push his people to hurry. There was nothing for them to do. Not until the Vanesco arrived. Then, if Bardon's little toy worked, there would be plenty to do. If it didn't, Mostyn didn't see any sense in continuing the mission. Dyer was right: if they couldn't see more than twenty feet, there wasn't much they could do in a vast open area.

Smithson picked up a handful of rock and soil. "No signs of any volcanism. These mountains must be the sole product of plate tectonics."

"Is that significant?" Baker asked.

"It might be," Smithson replied. "The distinctive features of Antarctica came about due to a lot of shoving and pushing, rather than a lot of fire and molten rock."

"Earthquakes, in other words," Baker said.

Smithson nodded. "Mostly."

"I wonder what the Elder Things thought of all that shaking?" Julia Pridmore asked of no one in particular.

"My uncle never mentioned anything about that," Terri Lynn Dyer replied. "Although you'd think it must've had some kind of impact on their society and their cities."

"You'd think," Pridmore said.

"What I find incredibly spooky," Amber Bailey said, "is how still it is here. No wind, no sound, nothing."

"Makes it easier for us to hear something trying to sneak up on us," Jones said.

"Except shoggoths don't make any sound," Dotty said.

"They make that weird piping and constantly repeat that obnoxious word," Sandy Schwartz corrected.

"That'd be a dead giveaway in this environment," NicAskill added.

The sound of an engine and tracks moving over rocks and earth came faintly to their ears.

"That should be Obermann and his toy," Mostyn said.

The sounds gradually grew louder and the vehicle's lights appeared.

Mostyn stood, held his flashlight over his head, and waved it back and forth. In response, the lights on the Vanesco went out and came back on. And in twenty minutes, the machine came to a halt next to the team members.

Obermann and Wulfe got out, and the doctor asked how they were going to do any exploring in the darkness.

"Wait and see," Mostyn replied.

A smile appeared on Jones's face. "The Boss has been holding out on us." To Mostyn, he said, "You have one of Doctor Bardon's toys, don't you?"

"Yes, I do, Jones. Yes, I do," Mostyn replied. "Come. Give me a hand."

14

THE TEAM WATCHED a beam of light shoot out of the smallish tripod-mounted cylinder. The beam touched the bottom of the ice ceiling thousands of feet above them, and like spilled milk flowing across the table, the light spread across the ceiling of ice and illuminated the Antarctic soil. What had been covered in a blanket of eternal night was now lit with a soft, unearthly, white light that had a slightly greenish tint to it.

"Oh, my God," Julia Pridmore said. "Look! That must be the city of the Elder Things."

All eyes turned in the direction she was pointing.

With wonderment and awe in her voice, Terri Lynn Dyer added, "Just like my uncle said."

A kilometer away, on the other side of a wide and now dry river bed, was a Cyclopean city that stretched for miles in either direction and lay roughly parallel to the mountain range.

The architecture was of a design never known to human

beings, and beyond human imagination, or human nightmares. The building material was stone, pitch-black in color, and the geometry of the structures, those truncated cones, those strange piles of stacked rectangular shapes, the tubular bridges and needle-like spires, and the persistently curious clustering of buildings in groups of five, was a monstrous perversion of any geometry ever conceived by human mathematicians.

There was an incredibly unhuman massiveness to the vast stone towers and crumbling ramparts that appeared to have once surrounded the city. And Mostyn thought that it was undoubtedly due to the massiveness, and that massiveness alone, that prevented the glaciers, that were spilling down from the Gamburtsevs, from destroying the city. Although, given enough time, he surmised, even the massive alien stronghold would have been no match for Nature's unrelenting onslaught.

Yet at some point the ice had vanished and left the city, along with the surrounding land, exposed to the still and silent air, and an eternal night. What was it that had caused the giant bubble to come into existence?

The city's architecture reminded Mostyn of comments Doctor Bardon had made regarding the demonic plateau of mysterious and forbidden Leng, or of his description of the unearthly Mi-Go and their coming to our solar system and this planet, or of the passages he'd read from the Pnakotic Manuscripts with their implication of the pre-human origin of the Cthulhu cult.

Mostyn came out of his reverie when he heard Helene telling the others of the impossibly ancient legends concerning Tsathoggua and the hideously formless star-spawn associated with that blasphemously evil entity.

While Helene told her stories, Mostyn took out his binoculars and surveyed the ramparts before them. Some forty-five million years ago the advancing glaciers, like a battering ram, had pushed the walls down. The gargantuan towers had withstood the ice and remained standing, but they had not stopped the advance of the ice. The ice sheet merely flowed around them. With the help of the binoculars, Mostyn could see the marks on the tower stones from the scouring effect of the ice.

Yet, at some point the ice had to have stopped. From what he could see, the ice sheet had not been higher than the tallest towers. Had the Elder Things somehow been able to slow or even stop the advance? Had they, in fact, created the bubble in which he and his team now stood? And where Doctor Dyer and his companion had stood all those many years ago?

Mostyn lowered his binoculars. The scene had a disquieting Roerich effect upon him, leaving him feeling a certain mystical uneasiness. He took a deep breath and exhaled, pushing the feelings of uneasiness aside. He addressed his team.

"Listen up, people We need to get a move on it. Courtesy of Doctor Bardon, the IDB XL-8 will give us twelve hours or so of light and then it will have to rest."

"Rest?" Doctor Heidegger said.

"Yes," Mostyn replied. "It is a class XL-8 Inter-Dimensional Being. The R and D people were able to translate the ancient summoning ritual into a computer algorithm. With the press of a button, the IDB will work for us, but only for twelve hours."

"What happens then, sir?" Amber Bailey asked.

"We're back in the dark," Mostyn answered. "So let's get a move on it. We have a kilometer to walk to get to the city."

"We could use the Vanesco," Obermann volunteered. "It would get us to the city faster than if we walked."

Mostyn took a moment to consider Obermann's suggestion and then nodded. "You make a valid point, Doctor. Very well. Everyone into the Vanesco. It'll be a tight squeeze, but we won't be sardines for long."

Jones put his arm around Helene. "Why can't Ms. Stealth here do her thing to ease the crowding?"

NicAskill and Mostyn both stood with hands on hips, glaring at Jones.

Helene giggled, and Jones disappeared. In a moment, his head reappeared above the frozen ground.

"What the...?" he spluttered.

The team burst out laughing.

"I think you were getting a little too fresh there, Jones," Baker said, while packing up the stove.

"I am a married woman, DC," Helene said.

"Okay, okay, I'm sorry," Jones said. "Get me outta here. Please."

And there, in a blink of an eye, Jones was standing on the frozen ground. "Whew. Thanks, Helene. I'm sorry. I didn't—"

Helene silenced him with a finger on his lips. "It is okay. We are still friends, DC Jones." She smiled. "I played a joke on you." She turned to Mostyn. "DC's idea is a good one, Mostyn Pierce."

"It is at that," Mostyn agreed. "Any volun—"

Before he could finish saying the word, Helene, Dotty, Terri Lynn Dyer, Julia Pridmore, and Amber Bailey vanished.

Mostyn looked around and finished saying the word "volunteers".

"I guess that's that," Baker said, clapping Mostyn on the shoulder, a big grin on his face.

"I guess it is," Mostyn said. "The rest of you, all aboard."

While his team members were getting on board the ice melting and boring machine, Mostyn looked at the city. In one of the supremely tall and enormously unhuman cylindrical towers, Mostyn saw a light with a yellow cast to it appear in what must have been a window.

He pulled his binoculars to his eyes, but by then the light was gone.

Jones, waiting for Mostyn, asked, "What is it, Boss?"

Mostyn slowly lowered the binoculars. Had he actually seen a light in that tower? And if so, why had it gone out so quickly? Then again, maybe it was simply his imagination.

He turned around. "Nothing, Jones." And from the look on Jones's face, Mostyn knew the Special Agent didn't believe him.

15

OBERMANN'S ICE melting and boring machine trundled across the Antarctic landscape, negotiating the dry river bed without a problem. Mostyn looked out the window at the terrain, rocky in places, carved smooth in others. Smithson probably had an explanation, but Mostyn didn't care. He just wanted to take in a sight that probably only two other human beings had ever seen: Doctor William Dyer and Danforth, one of Dyer's team members.

Mostyn noticed Baker was clicking the camera shutter as fast as the camera would allow. He was under a non-negotiable deadline. They all were. In less than twelve hours, darkness would return.

"This is absolutely incredible!" Smithson exclaimed. "My only regret is that I can't publicly brag about being one of the first people to touch Antarctic soil."

Baker snapped a photo. "One of the perks for getting the big bucks that you do."

"I think I'd rather have the glory," Smithson said.

"There's a catch twenty-two for you," Jones said.

"Yes," Doctor Wilfred Heidegger concurred. "None of what we do is for public consumption. We have sacrificed much to protect our world."

"And thanks to Doctor Bardon we get to see all this," NicAskill said.

"This is one time we aren't left in the dark," Jones quipped.

Mostyn returned his gaze to the scenery outside his window and found himself wondering when the bubble had occurred. Sometime after at least the initial phases of glaciation, to be sure. Was it, though, millions of years ago? Or was the bubble created more recently? And what had created it? Natural forces? Or had the Elder Things made an attempt to reverse the course of nature? Was the bubble a testimony to their success? And was the light he saw, or thought he saw, connected?

The machine stopped and Jones deposited one of the beacons that would guide them back should the light fail before they could get to the mountains. When the machine resumed its trek to the city, Mostyn twisted in his seat in an attempt to get a look at the mountain range behind them.

The Gamburtsevs are not overly tall for a mountain range. Roughly on par with the Alps. Making them taller than the Appalachians, but not as tall as the Rockies. Being buried in ice, the mountains showed no signs of erosion, and had very pointed and jagged peaks. At least the ones that were not buried in the top of the ice dome. In a way, they looked like big, black witch hats.

Mostyn also noticed some of those strange cuboid shapes, mentioned by Lovecraft, that dotted the sides of the mountains. Which meant that Doctor William Dyer had indeed seen what Mostyn himself was now looking at. The question that begged to be asked was how did Dyer get below the surface of the ice? Or was it a case of the mountains and the city being temporarily exposed by those very same forces that had pushed ancient R'lyeh above the surface of the Pacific and forever altered the life of Gustaf Johanson?

The machine stopped again, and Jones set out another beacon. He got back in and the Vanesco was on its way.

Mostyn looked at the broken ramparts. He and his people were cut off from the outside world. Their radio signals incapable of penetrating the two to three thousand feet of ice above them. What if the light he saw was not the motel owner keeping the light on for them? What if it was the capital T in trouble?

They were armed, and they'd been in tough spots before. They'd make it out of this one too, should trouble come a calling.

"We're almost to the rampart, Mr. Mostyn," Obermann said. "Do you want to stop? Or look for the remnants of a gate? Or should I drill a path for us?"

"How's our fuel, Doctor?" Mostyn asked.

"We'll probably need to find water to recharge the cells if we bore a path through the stone. Otherwise, we should have enough to get us back."

"Then let's stop and we'll find a way through the broken masonry on foot."

"Very good, Mr. Mostyn."

The Vanesco came to a stop, and everyone exited the vehicle. In a moment, Helene and the other women rematerialized.

"Hello, ladies," Mostyn said. "Enjoy the trip?"

"I found the experience very disconcerting," Special Forces Agent JoEllen Tamsworth said.

Doctor Dyer nodded her head in agreement. Special Forces Agent Amber Bailey, on the other hand, found being dematerialized "an almost spiritual" experience.

Mostyn continued, "Now that we're all here, let me have your attention. Jones. I want you, Schwartz, Doctor Heidegger, and Doctor Smithson to move off half a kilometer in that direction." He pointed to where he wanted Jones and his group to go. "You will enter the city and move forward, keeping me informed of what you are seeing."

"Will do, Boss." Jones turned to his teammates. "Let's stock up. Weapons, ammo, food, and water."

"Don't forget a heater," Mostyn added.

"Right," Jones replied.

Mostyn turned his attention to the remaining team members.

"Tamsworth, Helene, Doctor Dyer, and Doctor Obermann, you four will go with NicAskill. Position yourselves half a kilometer in that direction...," Mostyn pointed, "...and enter the city. Keep me informed of your progress and what you are seeing."

"Yes, sir," NicAskill said, and motioned for her team to follow her to the Vanesco for supplies.

To Wulfe, Mostyn said, "You'll stay here with our ticket home. Make sure it's ready to go should we need to leave in a hurry."

"Will do, Mr. Mostyn."

"That leaves the rest of you with me," Mostyn said. "Get your equipment and then we'll be moving into the city through this rubble that is before us."

"Thank goodness we have some climbing equipment," Dotty said. "These are some big blocks of stone."

"Like something out of Stonehenge," Baker quipped.

"These stones are much larger, I think, than those," Doctor Pridmore said.

"Lucky us," Dotty replied.

NicAskill and her team headed for their entry point. Mostyn and his people gathered their equipment, and when everyone was set, he slowly panned the Cyclopean ruins ahead of them with the binoculars.

Nothing. Just ruined masonry. Maybe that light was just a figment of his imagination. Maybe. *Then again*, he thought, *maybe the Pope is an atheist.*

16

THE TUMBLED down pile of stone that once comprised the city's wall in this spot was immense. Julia Pridmore speculated that the wall had probably been at least one hundred feet high. The blocks of primordial schist and slate were upwards of eight feet in length, six feet in width, and four feet thick. Although few were completely intact.

"It looks as though the glacier pushed the wall down," Pridmore said, "and then shoved the rubble a good two hundred feet before stopping."

Dotty, hands on hips, looked at the huge pile of broken stone. "What you're saying, Julia, is that climbing this rock pile is going to be a bitch."

Pridmore laughed. "Something like that."

Mostyn took a grappling hook out of his pack, attached a rope to it and swung the thing above his head several times before letting it fly towards the rock pile. It landed with a clank that was loud in the stillness of their sub-glacial world. Mostyn pulled on it and when it failed to catch, hauled it back.

A second and third throw also found the hook failing to secure itself in the rocks.

"Want me to give it a try, Mostyn?" Baker said.

"Sure, Willie Lee, give it a go."

Baker took the hook from Mostyn, swung it in a circle a few times to get some momentum, and let it fly. The hook landed with a clank. Baker pulled on the rope and was rewarded with a taut line.

"There you go, Boss," Baker said, taking a little bow.

"Thanks, Willie Lee," Mostyn replied. "I'll go first to make sure the line holds."

"Maybe the lightest one should go first, Mostyn," Dotty said.

Looking at the three women, Baker said, "I'm certainly the heaviest."

"I'll go," Mostyn said. "I'm the leader. Which means, I lead."

"Just be careful, will you?" Dotty said.

"I will, Dot. I don't want to make this my permanent home."

Mostyn clipped a carabiner to the belt around his waist and to the rope. Baker secured the rope end, so the line was relatively taut. Mostyn looped the rope around one gloved hand and began to climb up the rock pile.

His boots weren't designed for climbing and the rocks were slick with ice in spots, resulting in several slips and a banged shin before he was halfway to the hook. In spite of the pain, he pressed forward.

With only ten feet to go, Mostyn's foot slipped and got stuck in a space where three rocks came together. He let loose with an expletive and pulled. Nothing. He shook his head, looked over the situation, and tried turning his foot this way and that. Nothing.

He loosened his bootlaces and pulled his foot out of the boot, then worked the boot out of the hole.

Damn, it's cold, he thought. He massaged his foot to bring blood flow and warmth to it, and put his boot back on.

Dotty's voice sounded in his earpiece. "You okay up there, Mostyn?"

"Now I am," he replied. "The rocks wanted my boot."

"You got stuck?" Dotty replied. "With those little feet of yours?"

"Very funny, Kemper."

Her laughter rang in his ear.

Mostyn crossed the ten feet to where the grapnel was wedged in the broken masonry. He piled more rocks around it to make sure it would hold and signaled for the next person to come.

Fifty minutes passed before the last team member, Special Forces Agent Amber Bailey, finished climbing the pile of broken masonry. While his team was climbing up the Cyclopean ramparts, Mostyn climbed up the remaining fifteen feet to the top. Looking down the other side, a smile lifted his lips. Lady Luck had smiled on them, for there were four slabs that had tumbled in such a way as to form a sort of giant staircase on which they could ease their way down.

One by one, as Kemper, Pridmore, and Baker made their way to the top, Mostyn sent them down the other side. When Bailey arrived, he sent her down and followed.

Standing inside the ancient ruin, Mostyn looked at the piles of rubble. They were all that remained of the buildings near the wall. He turned his gaze towards the gargantuan structures deeper in the city that were still standing. The pyramids and truncated cones. The tall cylinders and tubular bridges, a few of which remained in place. The cuboid structures of various sizes and positions. The minaret-like towers, and everywhere the five-pointed star pattern.

In addition, to Mostyn's eye, and when he mentioned it to the others they agreed, there was a certain alien quality to the angles and perspectives, which when viewed with the human eye gave the viewer a certain sense of uneasiness and a dysphoria that made the skin goosebump.

Dotty Kemper summed up the feeling when she said, "It's like you need glasses looking at this place. Everything is slightly out of focus, and after a while it gives you a headache. It just isn't normal."

"Okay, people, let's move forward," Mostyn said, "and keep your eyes and ears open. We've encountered one shoggoth. There may be others."

And as if in response to Mostyn's statement, in the distance, disrupting the stillness and silence, they heard a piping sound with a distinctly unearthly quality to it that modulated over a wide range.

17

"THAT WASN'T CAUSED by the wind," Dotty said.

"Because there isn't any," Baker added.

The look on Mostyn's face was grim. He keyed his mic. "Jones. NicAskill. You copy that piping sound?"

"I did, Boss," Jones answered.

NicAskill also indicated she and her group had heard it.

"Be alert. Those things are cunning."

A mirthless chuckle sounded. Jones said, "Cunning isn't the word for it. We'll be careful."

"I'm not partial to slime," NicAskill added. "We'll be alert. Very alert."

"Good," Mostyn said. "You two have any trouble getting into the city?"

Jones said his team had minimal problems and NicAskill added that Helene had simply dematerialized them and they walked through the rubble.

Mostyn repeated his command to be alert and signed

off. He began walking, and with a hand signal indicated his team should follow.

The piping had stopped as quickly as it had begun, and the silence once again became deafening, relieved only by the sound of booted feet on paving stones.

Baker was busy taking pictures, and Julia Pridmore murmured a running commentary into her digital recorder. Dotty walked with Mostyn, the two of them scanning the buildings for anything that might appear unusual. Although, given that all of it was unusual, they had no idea what that unusual thing they were looking for might be.

Following the four was Special Forces Agent Amber Bailey. She, too, was listening and looking for anything that might not fit into a setting where nothing fit. And there, in the upper-story window of a building that was surprisingly well-preserved, she saw a light. A light with a yellow tint to it that made it stand out from the greenish cast of the IDB XL-8.

She pointed and called out, "Up there, a light."

Four pairs of eyes followed her pointing finger.

Baker, sweeping the building with his camera, said, "I don't see anything."

"It was there. I saw it," Bailey insisted.

"I believe you," Mostyn said. "I saw a light, too, in one of the buildings before we even entered the city."

"And you're only telling us this now, Mostyn?" Dotty was clearly perturbed. "Didn't you think that was some-thing you should maybe share with your *team*?"

"It disappeared so quickly I wasn't even sure I saw it," he replied.

"Maybe we should check out the building," Bailey said. "If something is there, we don't want it behind us."

Mostyn thought for but a moment. "Yes, let's check out the building. Best if we know what we're up against. If anything."

The building was some three hundred feet in front of them. They took their time walking to the gargantuan structure, keeping alert for any movement or sound that might indicate they had company.

Some twenty feet in front of the doors, Mostyn signaled for the team to stop. His gaze slowly moved up the structure that was undoubtedly ancient before humans or their predecessors even existed. A truncated cone some fifty stories tall had been built on top of a two-story star-shaped base.

He eyeballed each story and guessed the height to be about thirty feet for each one. Making the structure some fifteen to sixteen hundred feet tall. And it was nowhere near the tallest building in the city.

Dotty looked up towards the top of the building, and, with hands on hips, said, "I don't suppose this place has an elevator."

"Probably not in working order," Baker replied.

"Why doesn't Bardon give us something useful, like a magic elevator?" she said.

"Climbing the stairs will keep you fit," Mostyn told her, to which Dotty gave him a look that would have melted ice if any had been nearby.

He mounted the ramp, proceeded to the large doors,

and opened one. "Glad they didn't lock up the store when they left."

The inside of the building was dimly lit by the outside light filtering in through the windows. The headlamps and wrist lamps did little to further illuminate the interior gloom.

To their right and left ran a wide corridor, each end disappearing into the murky darkness. Windows punctuated the exterior wall at regular intervals. The interior wall was covered with murals, but otherwise featureless. The ceiling was about fifteen feet above them, and was polished stone, their lamps gleaming back at them from the smooth surface.

"Let's see if we can find some stairs," Mostyn said, and set off walking clockwise along the inner wall.

"I wonder if the mural on this wall is a retelling of their history, or if it's a retelling of mythological stories connected with their religion?" Julia Pridmore asked of no one in particular.

Baker took photographs of the wall section Pridmore was looking at.

Mostyn looked back. "Difficult to say. Don't get separated, you two."

Baker took another photo, and the two jogged to catch up to the group.

"This building is in surprisingly good condition when you figure it could be fifty million or more years old, given what we know about these Elder Things," Pridmore said.

"I doubt anything people have built will last that long," Dotty added.

"I wonder, though," Mostyn said, "if this city would have survived if it hadn't been buried in the ice."

"Good point, Agent Mostyn," Pridmore replied.

"The Elder Things apparently built cities all over the world, but this one is the only one we know about," Mostyn continued.

"So what you're saying," Pridmore said, "is that not even these advanced beings could build something to withstand the forces of nature."

"That's what I'm saying," Mostyn replied.

"It's like nature is the casino and all life forms are the gamblers," Dotty said. "The house always wins."

"Geez, Kemper, must you always be so negative?" Baker asked.

"Tell me one thing I should be optimistic about," Dotty said.

"Everything," Baker shot back. "It's all in your attitude."

Dotty blew him a raspberry.

"Here we go, gang," Mostyn said, pointing to an opening in the wall.

"Interesting," Pridmore said. "A ramp instead of stairs."

"Given their five-pointed star-shaped pseudo-foot, a ramp makes more sense than stairs," Dotty explained. "Like the ramp mentioned by Schwartz back in the cave, and the one we used to enter this building."

Pridmore nodded.

They took the ramp up to the second floor, the layout of which looked to be a repeat of the first floor. The ramp continued its climb and Mostyn decided to follow it.

On what would have been the third floor, the walls fell away from the ramp and it appeared to float in the air.

"We must be in the cone part of the building," Pridmore said.

The center of the building, which was to their left, was open space, their lights not picking up any sign of a wall. To their right was a floor and rooms, with windows and doorways.

Mostyn stepped off the ramp and shone his light onto the wall which separated the rooms from the rest of the building. The black stone, which seemed the common building material, reflected back the light of his flashlight beam. His light revealed a window and a doorway. A greenish-white glow came from inside the room.

"There must be a window on the outside wall," Dotty said.

"How are we going to check out all these rooms?" Amber Bailey asked. "This place is huge, and we only have, what, about nine hours of outside light left?"

And, as if in answer to her question, they heard an unearthly flute-like piping modulating over a wide tonal range.

18

WITHOUT WARNING, the interior of the building was ablaze with light, although where it emanated from no one on Mostyn's team was able to determine.

Now that it was illuminated, Mostyn and his people looked in awe at the vast interior layout of the tall tower. What they saw was an immense open space, with rooms lining the outside walls, and the vastness just went up and up.

Mostyn marveled at what was an incredible feat of engineering. The rampway was open on either side, but was anchored to each of the floors that circled the outside wall of the alien skyscraper.

However, what quickly drew their attention away from the incredible architecture was the spectacle that was taking place high above where the team was standing.

Five Elder Things, their wings beating the air as they hovered or made lazy circles of the interior, were making piping sounds that covered an incredibly wide tonal range.

Somewhat below them were two groups of shoggoths on opposite sides of the wide expanse. The smaller group of five was silent. The other group, numbering a dozen, was repeating "Tekeli-li!" over and over without pause.

The Elder Things were carrying strange looking tube-like objects in their tentacles. One of the beings piped a certain pattern of notes. A split second later, the smaller group charged towards the larger. At the same time the Elder Things aimed their tube-like objects at the larger group. There was a brief oscillating high-pitched sound and five of the shoggoths vaporized moments before the two groups crashed together and tore into each other.

Mostyn watched the shoggoth battle, and noticed one of the iridescent black spheres had separated from the others and changed its shape into something resembling a net, and hurtled itself towards the group of Elder Things.

One of the Elder Things fired its weapon at the charging creature. The alien apparently missed because a moment later the black net surrounded the being, transformed itself back into a sphere, and dropped to the floor below.

Two of the Elder Things flew in pursuit, swooped down on the rapidly rolling shoggoth, and disintegrated the unearthly blasphemy of nature with their weapons. There was no sign of the Elder Thing the shoggoth had captured, and Mostyn assumed it too had been disintegrated. *Perhaps,* he thought, *the Elder Things figured their companion was already dead.*

Meanwhile, the mass of amoeboid obscenities was slowly revolving and undulating. It was impossible for Mostyn to tell which group was winning, as they were so entangled the creatures looked like one massively foul and unwholesome entity, with eyes and mouths rapidly appearing and disappearing.

The four remaining Elder Things aimed their weapons at the massive sphere. There was the brief oscillating high-pitched sound and the entire mass of shoggoths vanished.

"That's some weapon they have there, sir," Bailey said.

Mostyn nodded. "Must be a disruptor similar to our sonic disruptor."

"Only much more advanced. Not as clunky as ours."

"That's for sure."

Mostyn keyed his mic to the team's open channel. "Attention. Mostyn here. Have encountered Elder Things and shoggoths."

"Those things are heading our way, Mostyn."

"I see that, Kemper," Mostyn replied. He continued, "Elder Things have disruptor-type weapon, and have spotted us. I'll leave this channel open. Be prepared to fall back and get to the surface."

One of the Elder Things landed in front of Mostyn and his team. The other three remained in the air. The being that landed pointed its weapon at Mostyn and commenced a stream of piping sounds.

In response, Mostyn raised his hands in the universal sign language of surrender. He just hoped it was universal in whatever universe the Elder Things came from.

19

"WE MUST HELP THEM," Helene said.

"I don't think there's anything we can do," NicAskill replied, while looking at the tracking screen on her tablet. "They're almost a kilometer from where we are, and we don't know what's between us and them. Which means we can't hurry."

"We must save my husband and my sister," Helene said.

"We're not a combat force, Helene," NicAskill replied.

Over the open mic, they heard piping sounds, but no human speech.

"If my uncle was right, these things look at us the same way we look at insects," Terri Lynn Dyer said. "We probably can't get there fast enough to be of any help."

A defiant Helene spat out, "I will rescue my husband and sister." And before anyone could blink, she vanished.

Looking at the tracking screen on his tablet, Jones said, "They're only two-thirds of a kilometer from us."

"Will we get there in time?" Daniel Smithson asked.

"Don't know. Don't care." Jones replied. "They need our help. Let's go."

Jones took off at a trot, the rest of his group following. He keyed his mic for NicAskill. "Nicky, we're moving in to attempt rescue."

He heard back, "Are you crazy, Jones? Mostyn didn't tell us to rescue him."

"He didn't," Jones agreed. "But he's the boss, and he needs rescuing."

"That crazy Helene vanished and is on her way."

"Go, Ms. Stealth!"

"You're crazy, Jones, you know that? We need to go back."

"I'm the senior officer, NicAskill," Jones replied. "We're rescuing our teammates. No one gets left behind."

"Goddamn it, Jones." There was a pause, and then he heard, "Very well. We're on our way."

————

Jones, Schwartz, Heidegger, and Smithson were halfway to the building where Mostyn had encountered the Elder Things when he noticed the blips on his tablet, representing Mostyn, Bailey, Kemper, Baker, and Pridmore, had started moving. He radioed NicAskill.

"I see them, Jonesy. They're heading in my direction."

"Can you intercept?" Jones asked.

"Not wise. I only have Tamsworth who is combat ready."

"Position yourself on the right flank and shadow them. We'll move in on the left."

"Gotcha. Will do."

Mostyn shuddered. The Elder Things were horrific looking entities that emitted a fetidly foul stench. To him, their look and smell was befitting for an alien form of life, a life form not even native to this universe. One that for all intents and purposes was hostile to human existence.

The body of the Elder Things was six to seven feet tall, barrel-shaped, and three to four feet wide at the middle. Adding head and feet, they were easily eight feet or more in height. Their color was a uniform light gray.

On their backs were two wings, with a wingspan of at least fourteen feet.

The head was shaped like a starfish and was attached to a short neck. On each of the points was a red-irised eye. In the center of the head was an opening that Mostyn guessed must serve as a mouth. Each creature had five arms. Each arm had five branches and on each branch were five tentacles. Each creature had five four foot long tentacle-like appendages attached to the five-pointed base and each appendage ended in a triangular-shaped paddle. These served as legs and feet for the Elder Things. Their movement was a sort of coordinated undulation, or slithering like that of a snake. The Things wore no clothes.

After Mostyn and his people had raised their hands in surrender, the Elder Things conferred amongst themselves for some time before coming to a decision. What that decision was, Mostyn didn't know. He hoped it didn't bode ill for him and his team.

One of the Elder Things started moving and another pointed at it. Mostyn said to his people, "Looks like we're to follow them. Keep alert. Their ignorance of us and our anatomy and letting us keep our equipment and weapons is a good thing."

There was a string of flute-like notes, followed by one of the Elder Things pointing its weapon at Mostyn.

"Okay, okay," he said. "I get it. Shut up and follow." But the question in his mind was why were they walking instead of flying?

———

NicAskill held up her hand, and her team stopped trotting. A piping sound, modulating over a wide tonal range, reached their ears. She looked at her tablet. The five blips representing Mostyn and his team were a block or two away.

She showed the image on the tablet to Tamsworth, Dyer, and Obermann. "They're close. Tamsworth and I will move in closer to get a look at what we're up against." Pointing to Dyer and Obermann, she added, "You two wait here. We'll be back as soon as we can. But if we aren't back in twenty, return to the Vanesco."

Obermann and Dyer nodded.

NicAskill and Tamsworth trotted down the street, keeping close to the buildings.

"I wonder if these Elder Things had cars?" Tamsworth asked.

"Good question. The streets are wide enough."

The two rounded a corner. The piping grew louder, and NicAskill put out a hand to stop Tamsworth. Hugging the side of a building, they saw one of the Elder Things come into view, followed by Mostyn, Kemper, Baker, Pridmore, and Bailey. On either side of the line of humans was one of the Things. The fourth was slithering along some distance behind Bailey, who was last in the line.

Tamsworth whispered, "Not good odds, Nicky. Two of us against four of them."

"No. However, if Mostyn, Bailey, and Kemper could get to their weapons…" She paused a moment, and then came to a decision. "We'll shadow them and wait for Jones to catch up. Go and get the doctors. Meet me at the next block up."

Tamsworth gave her a thumbs up and took off down the street.

I wonder if I can cut through this building to get to the next block? NicAskill asked herself.

She tested the door and found it unlocked. She slowly pulled it open and took one more look at the slowly moving column.

The air behind the last Elder Thing shimmered, and NicAskill whispered, "Oh, shit."

Helene had rematerialized.

20

JONES LOOKED at the dots on his tablet. There were the five which made up Mostyn's team. He saw the two dots near Mostyn's group and guessed those were NicAskill and Tamsworth.

At this point, he didn't want to risk calling NicAskill. She was too close to the aliens, assuming they were with Mostyn, and he didn't know how good their hearing was. He hoped his guess was correct. When he was in position, another minute or so, then he'd contact his partner.

Jones motioned for everyone to move towards the buildings on their left. Best not to be in the middle of the street should any shooting start.

He watched one of the blips move away, and then a new blip appeared on the screen.

I'll bet my entire pension that's Helene, he thought.

"Come on, let's step on it," he said in a loud whisper to his three teammates. "Things are about to heat up."

———

Some twenty feet behind the last Elder Thing, Helene rematerialized. The creature's head was tilted forward and the five eyes were focused forward and to the sides.

Helene stepped softly so as not to attract attention. She marveled at the size of the alien being. For even though she was a tall woman, the immense size of the being dwarfed her. Legends were one thing. Real life another.

She thought, *What is the best way to surprise this thing?*

An idea came to her and she once again dematerialized. She sent a thought message to Mostyn and the team members with him telling them to be prepared to attack when she distracted the Elder Things.

She rematerialized a mere two feet behind the creature who was the rear guard and fired her pistol point blank into the back of the head of the Elder Thing.

———

When Mostyn heard Helene in his mind, he smiled. They just might make it home after all. He reached down and unsnapped the strap holding his tactical knife in its sheath.

In a moment, he had his plan of attack. He had no understanding of his captor's interior anatomy. However, if a being has a head and a body, it's reasonable to assume communication between the head and the body passes through the neck. Therefore, the neck was the best place to attack. Disrupt that communication.

At the sound of the gunshot, Mostyn leaped onto the back of the Elder Thing in front of him. He wrapped his legs around the thing's middle and his left arm held onto the thing's head.

The knife in his right hand plunged into the alien's neck. The tough, leathery skin was difficult to get through. A green ooze began flowing out of the wound. The creature's tentacles grasped at him, trying to pull him off.

Mostyn gritted his teeth and pushed the knife blade into the thing's neck all the way to the handle. Pulling back on the head with his left hand and pushing the knife forward with his right, Mostyn tried to cut through as much of the thing's neck as possible.

The creature emitted a high-pitched piping, which died in a gurgling sound. The being's tentacles grasped at Mostyn. The alien was strong, and Mostyn felt himself being pulled off the creature's back.

Somewhere on the edge of his consciousness he was aware of screams and piping and yelling and gunshots and the whine of the disruptor. He pulled out the knife and plunged it into the front of the thing's neck. He pulled it out and plunged it in again. The green ooze was spraying and flowing out of the thing's wounds.

Mostyn felt the tentacles tighten and the alien pulled him from off its back. But it couldn't hold on to him and Mostyn slipped out of its grasp, fell to the pavement, rolled, and came up onto his feet. He pulled out his pistol and sent six forty-five caliber bullets into the Elder Thing's head. Green ooze and leathery flesh sprayed out the back. The giant alien being swayed as if in a breeze and then fell over backwards.

Mostyn took in the scene on the street. The Elder Things were dead. NicAskill was trying to calm a hysterical Julia Pridmore, and Dotty Kemper was doing something to Baker's shoulder. From what Mostyn could see, it looked as though the photographer's shoulder was dislocated. As Dotty worked on it, Baker's scream confirmed Mostyn's suspicion.

He walked over to a now calmer Doctor Pridmore. NicAskill stood.

"She going to be all right?" Mostyn asked.

"I think so," NicAskill responded. "I think she just overloaded."

"She's not new. Been around for a while."

NicAskill shrugged. "We all have our tipping point. I guess she found hers."

Mostyn knelt down, said a few words to Pridmore, and then stood.

Jones and his team members rounded a corner at a full run, and came to a stop when they saw the humans were alive.

"Glad you could make it to the party, Jones," Mostyn called out.

"We got here as fast as we could."

"Thank you for thinking of us." Mostyn turned to NicAskill. "Where's Tamsworth, Dyer, and Obermann?"

"They'll be here shortly, sir."

Mostyn nodded and walked to each one of the dead Elder Things. He made a quick study of how each of the aliens had died. One was buried face down in the frozen pavement. Only its wings were visible. Another had died from Helene's well-placed gunshot. And then there was the one he himself had killed. The fourth one must've been disintegrated by the disruptor.

Tamsworth, Dyer, and Obermann ran around a corner and headed towards the group. Tamsworth was yelling, "Shoggoths!", over and over again.

And running in counterpoint to Tamsworth's yelling could be heard, "Tekeli-li! Tekeli-li!"

MOSTYN POINTED towards a building and told his team to set up a defensive position inside. Once inside, though, they discovered there wasn't anything that could be used as a barricade.

Next to the large double doors was a window without glass.

"This isn't a good position, Boss," Jones said.

"No, it isn't. We'll have to make do," Mostyn replied.

"Right," Jones said. He directed Tamsworth, armed with the E-753 chlorine trifluoride "shoggoth killer," to hold the doors, and positioned Bailey and Schwartz to hold the large open window. Bailey was armed with the grenade launcher, and Schwartz, the sonic disruptor.

Mostyn went to the window, leaning out to get a look down the street. The word "Tekeli-li," coming from a chorus of voices, was loud on the still air. And then he saw them: three massive iridescent spheres, eyes and mouths appearing and disappearing all over their bodies as they rolled down the street.

"Bailey." Mostyn pointed at the lead shoggoth.

"Yes, sir?"

"Grenade. Now!"

She pointed the grenade launcher and pulled the trigger. The small thermite bomb landed in front of the lead shoggoth and in a brilliant flash of intense heat and flame, rapidly incinerated the protoplasmic monstrosity.

The other two enormous creatures broke apart, something like when an orange is broken apart into segments. In their place, were a dozen smaller, yet still huge entities.

Bailey reloaded with a Bardonite grenade and fired again. The cylinder sailed into the midst of the alien beings and exploded in a shower of chemicals. Five of the shoggoths began changing colors and rolled around in circles, screaming high-pitched sounds, until they were reduced to viscous puddles that quickly froze in the frigid temperatures.

Schwartz fired the odd 1930s science fiction looking sonic disruptor and was rewarded with one of the shoggoths vanishing. The remaining six monstrosities rolled towards Mostyn, Schwartz, and Bailey, gaining speed the closer they came.

Mostyn tapped Bailey's arm and Schwartz's shoulder, motioning for them to fall back. He followed, calling out, "Here they come!"

The shoggoths lined up opposite the building where Mostyn and his team had sought refuge, and one sent a long pseudopod with an eye on it, across the street, and through the open window. Tamsworth turned the E-753 on the thing and sprayed the eye with chlorine trifluoride. The end of the pseudopod sizzled and melted away. A high-pitched piping immediately started up.

Jones laughed. "That thing is probably cussing us out in shoggoth."

"Do they even have a language?" NicAskill asked.

"They have to communicate somehow," Baker replied, while Dotty fashioned a sling for his left arm.

A shoggoth came rolling towards the window. Schwartz aimed the sonic disruptor at the thing and pulled the trigger. There was a high-pitched whine and then the shoggoth came apart. It hung in the air, a cloud of minute particles, and then slowly drifted to the street.

"Five to go," Mostyn said. "Bailey, send another grenade out there."

"Yes, sir." She pointed the grenade launcher and pulled the trigger. The grenade sped towards a shoggoth. The creature, seemingly anticipating Bailey's move, divided itself in two. The grenade flew between the two monstrosities, through the open window of the building behind them, and exploded in a mini-inferno. The two shoggoths then reformed as one.

"Well, I'll be...," Bailey said. "Those things are smart."

"That's why they ended up killing their masters," Doctor Heidegger said.

"Two of the things just left," Bailey said.

"And there go two more," Schwartz added.

"They're up to something," Mostyn said.

"You think they're trying to surround us?" Jones asked.

"Got it in one, Jones," Mostyn replied. "You and Tamsworth see if this place has a back door."

"On it, Boss," Jones said, heading for the back of the building with JoEllen Tamsworth.

"We can't just sit here," Julia Pridmore said, her voice sounding on the edge of hysteria.

Mostyn moved next to her. "Where do you suggest we go, Julia?"

"Anywhere. Anywhere but here."

"I'm working on that. Just leave it to me, okay?"

She looked at Mostyn. "You are?"

"Yes, I am."

She looked away and nodded.

Jones returned. "There is a back door, and I left Tams guarding it." He looked out the window. "Just that one?"

"Just that one," Mostyn confirmed.

Yet, while they watched, the shoggoth divided itself into two.

"Well, I'll be damned," Jones said.

"Looks like they're hellbent on making things complicated for us," Mostyn added.

"Maybe we ought to chance making a break for the Vanesco," Jones suggested. "We're just sitting ducks here."

"Been thinking the same thing," Mostyn replied. "We only have about six hours of light left."

"So maybe make our escape sooner rather than later."

"We need to take care of these two out front, or try slipping out the back."

"We know the situation and the streets out front. Don't know what things are like at the back of the building."

Mostyn thought a moment on what Jones had said and then nodded. "Let's see if we can't take care of these two bad boys out front and then get the hell out of here."

22

With Special Forces Agent Amber Bailey at the window, her grenade launcher aimed at the two alien entities, Mostyn, NicAskill, and Schwartz opened the doors and stepped outside. The two shoggoths, repeating "Tekeli-li" without ceasing, began rolling towards the humans the moment they were on the sidewalk.

Predictable as fizz in a pop bottle, Mostyn thought, then yelled, "Now!"

Schwartz dropped to a prone position, while Mostyn and NicAskill hurled their thermite grenades, one to the right of the creatures and one to the left, and hit the pavement.

The creatures moved into each other, and that's when Schwartz pulled the trigger on the sonic disruptor.

In a fraction of a second, the two anomalies of Newton's laws were vaporized, reduced to an invisible cloud of sub-atomic particles.

Mostyn jumped up and went back into the building. "Jones. Get Tamsworth. The rest of you, let's go."

The team filed out of the building and got into a loose formation. When Jones and Tamsworth rejoined the team, he and Mostyn took the lead. Tamsworth and Schwartz formed the rear guard, while NicAskill and Bailey were in the middle of the formation with the scientists.

They marched down the street at a brisk pace, Mostyn keeping an eye on the homing signal coming from the Vanesco.

"How long till we get to the bus for home?" Jones asked Mostyn.

"I think we're looking at twenty minutes, maybe more, to the wall, and then another half an hour to negotiate climbing over the rubble, and then another ten or so to the vehicle. Why?"

"Because there are four unaccounted for shoggoths. They could pop up anywhere. Just like a video game."

Mostyn let out a laugh. "We'll be lucky if those four are the only ones we have to deal with."

From behind them came a chorus of piping over a wide tonal range interspersed with "Tekeli-li."

"You jinxed us, Jones," Mostyn said, taking off at a run to the back of the formation. To his team, he yelled, "Scatter!"

Dotty, the other academics, and Baker ran to find cover. Helene dematerialized.

Mostyn watched five iridescent black spheres, eyes and mouths appearing and disappearing, roll down the street at high speed.

"Get ready," Mostyn said in a loud voice. "On my command."

The shoggoths raced towards the humans. One hundred feet. Seventy-five feet. Fifty feet.

"Now!" Mostyn yelled.

Mostyn, Jones, and NicAskill hurled thermite grenades and hit the pavement. Bailey pulled the trigger on the grenade launcher and a Bardonite chemical grenade shot into the midst of the charging shoggoths. Schwartz pulled the trigger on the sonic disruptor and Tamsworth on the chlorine trifluoride "shoggoth killer."

The shoggoths disappeared in a flaming inferno, except for one. That one bounced into the air, evading the streams of chlorine trifluoride and water, and with a gaping mouth and two tentacle-like pseudopods extended dropped down on Tamsworth, and at the same time wrapped a tentacle around Schwartz and ripped his head off.

Then the blasphemous agglutination of protoplasmic bubbles disappeared, and moments later Helene appeared in its place. The slime covered body of JoEllen Tamsworth lay on the pavement. Her head was nowhere to be seen.

"The creature is gone, Mostyn Pierce, but more are coming," Helene said.

Mostyn scratched his head. "I thought you couldn't dematerialize these things."

"They are difficult, but not impossible. This one was not so, how do you say..." After a moment she said, "So loosely formed, because it was killing our people."

"I see. Well, thanks."

He looked at his two dead teammates, but had no time

to express any sorrow at their loss, for Helene announced, "They are here, Mostyn Pierce."

Rolling down the street was an immense shoggoth that looked to be fifty feet in diameter. In a booming voice, it uttered "Tekeli-li!" over and over.

"Oh shit," Jones said, "we're in the soup now."

NicAskill picked up the sonic disruptor, flipped the selector to wide angle, and aimed it at the fast approaching monstrosity.

Shadow after shadow swept over Mostyn and his team mates. He looked up and saw two groups of five Elder Things heading for the oncoming behemoth, which changed its shape from a simple giant sphere to one that radiated long pseudopods, which reached out towards the oncoming Elder Things. Before the tentacle-like pseudopods could reach the alien beings, NicAskill and the aliens fired their weapons. The hideous thing vanished, leaving in its place a slight discoloration of the pavement.

Mostyn watched one group of Elder Things fly off. The other landed in a circle around Mostyn's team, their weapons pointed at the humans.

23

MOSTYN RAISED HIS HANDS, and the other members of his team did likewise. All except Helene, Dotty, and NicAskill. They were nowhere to be seen.

This time the Elder Things made it clear, Mostyn and his people were to drop their weapons and equipment.

Mostyn wasn't sure what the aliens knew and didn't know about humans. He figured it wouldn't hurt to find out and dropped the visible equipment to the pavement, but left his hidden backup pistol and knife in place. He noticed Jones and Bailey did the same.

The five Elder Things formed a cordon around Mostyn and the nine team members with him. Using rudimentary sign language, the things began herding the humans to the west.

They must have some manner of base on the west end of the city, Mostyn thought. *Which is going to put us some distance from the Vanesco.*

He sent his thoughts to Helene. *It's up to you, Dotty, and*

NicAskill. If you can't free us, get back to the surface as fast as possible.

In his mind came her answer. *Yes, Mostyn Pierce, my husband. Dotty and I love you.*

Mostyn sent back the thought that he loved them too, then turned his attention to the problem at hand. He was curious why the aliens didn't just fly them to wherever they were going. *Perhaps,* he thought, *they can't carry that much weight and fly at the same time.*

He also wondered if the Elder Things had a form of hive mind. What else would explain this group of Elder Things having them drop their weapons and equipment, when the previous group didn't? It was the only thing he could think of that made sense. And if that was the case, then they'd only be able to get the jump on the star-headed aliens once. Which more or less meant they had one chance to make good their escape, before their captors integrated the new information.

———

Helene, Dotty, and NicAskill waited until the aliens and their teammates were some distance ahead of them, to make sure the Elder Things had no interest in retrieving the equipment they'd forced the humans to drop, before rematerializing to pick up as much of the equipment as they could carry.

NicAskill was especially adamant that they take the grenade launcher, sonic disruptor, and the E-753 "shoggoth killer," although she wasn't overly impressed with the latter weapon.

"You want a weapon that uses water? In Antarctica?" Dotty shook her head.

"Something's better than nothing," she said to Dotty, who replied, "Whatever," and picked up a backpack.

With their teammates and their captors some three hundred feet ahead of them, NicAskill, Dotty, and Helene, followed, walking in line and close to the buildings lining the street.

"I wonder where they are taking them?" Dotty asked.

The other two couldn't answer her question. Although, like Mostyn, NicAskill speculated the Elder Things had a base on the west side of the city.

Dotty checked her watch. They had less than five hours of light left. When she mentioned the fact to the others, NicAskill said, "I hope our flashlights and lamps hold out, because if the lights go out before we've reached the Vanesco, we'll die here."

"I have never been in a place where there was no light," Helene said. "We always have light in K'n-yan."

"Yeah, well you aren't in K'n-yan anymore," Dotty said. "And for all intents and purposes, we're in a fricking cave with no natural light. Now there's a new experience for you."

After a moment, Helene said, "I think you are making fun of me, my sister."

"Touché. And I'm not your sister."

NicAskill looked at her two companions, and asked,

"It's probably none of my business, but how do you two get along with the boss?"

Helene started to speak but was cut off by Dotty. "You're right: it's none of your business. But if you want to know, ask Bardon."

NicAskill decided that was a good place to leave the conversation and pointed to the Elder Things and their prisoners. "We better pick up the pace here."

The minutes stretched into an hour before the three women began seeing evidence of the Elder Things's base. Helene dematerialized herself and the other two so they would not be seen by the Elder Things.

They began noticing guards on rooftops and in windows, both Elder Things and shoggoths. And when they followed the aliens and their teammates around a corner, there was a large version of the alien's hand-held weapon, mounted on a tripod, positioned in the middle of the street.

I think we've arrived, NicAskill told the other two by sending her thoughts to them. *Be observant, so we know what we're up against and how to get back to our ride home.*

The women watched the Elder Things take their prisoners to a building. Mostyn, Jones, Baker, and the professors filed inside and two of the aliens stood guard outside the door.

Let us now join our team, Helene thought out to her companions.

I'd rather slit a few throats, Dotty replied.

All in due time, Doctor Kemper, NicAskill thought. *All in due time.*

24

THE ELDER THINGS herded Mostyn and his team into a building. It appeared to be a smallish two-story structure. Resembling what Mostyn thought would be an Elder Thing house. He and his team were in a largish room. Perhaps their equivalent of a living room. There was no furniture. Straight ahead was a hallway, and to the right of the hall was a ramp that Mostyn assumed went to the upper floor.

Two of the aliens guarded the ramp, and the remaining Elder Things left. However, a look out the front window told Mostyn what he'd suspected. Guards. Two of them.

From what he knew of the Elder Things, Mostyn wondered why they'd been taken prisoner in the first place. As he understood the supposed history, the beings had created all manner of life forms after coming to Earth. Humans being one of those myriad species. At the same time, the aliens seemed to have little concern about their creations once they'd come into being.

So why not just exterminate us? he asked himself. The only conclusion that made any sense, to Mostyn at least, was that the beings either wanted to discover how advanced humans had become, which would explain their interest in the morgue, or they wanted information as to how the humans had been able to get to the city.

Whichever it was, he didn't have time to speculate. He needed to discover if there was a way out, and if so how they'd get out.

Mostyn walked down the hall to the back of the ground floor. Along the way he passed a doorway on either side of the hall. He took a look in each room, musing on the spare use of doors by the Elder Things, for neither entrance had one. The rooms were empty, and he moved on to the largish room at the back of the building.

It was empty, like the front room, and had a doorway, with no door, that opened into a fifth empty room, and a door that Mostyn guessed opened out onto a back street, or perhaps a yard. He checked the door, found it wasn't locked, but when he opened it, saw that two more Elder Things stood guard.

"They aren't taking any chances," Mostyn muttered to himself while closing the door, noting that it opened out onto another street.

He turned around, intending to join the others who were clustered in the front room, when Helene, Dotty, and NicAskill materialized in front of him. Mostyn was surprised, however years of discipline had taught him silence was golden and he made no sound.

Dotty passed his weapons to him, while Helene's voice sounded in his mind: *we will get you and the others out.* And then the three vanished.

Mostyn hid the weapons in the pockets of his parka and rejoined his team. "There are guards on the front and back doors," he announced. "Two each. Plus the two guards over there. However, all is not lost. We have our three friendly Caspers, if you know what I mean. We'll be on our way home soon."

The front door opened and three Elder Things entered. Two had disruptors. The third had nothing that appeared to be a weapon, at least as near as Mostyn could tell.

The Elder Thing, without any obvious weapon showing, turned its large star-shaped head from one side of the room to the other. Five eyes taking in Mostyn's team.

In Mostyn's mind, a picture formed. There was a human and the other humans were bowing down before him. Mostyn chuckled. *Helene should be here*, he thought, *telepathy is her thing*.

The picture faded out, and another took its place. This one had Mostyn standing and everyone bowing down to him.

A smile flashed across Mostyn's face. They want to know if I'm the leader. He thought for a moment and decided he wasn't going to tell them anything. After all, he had no idea what they might do to him in order to extract information. He put a blank look on his face and let his two eyes stare down the five eyes of the alien.

The Elder Thing turned away and focused its attention

on Julia Pridmore. Only a few seconds passed before she raised her arm and pointed at Mostyn.

He lowered his head and slowly shook it from side to side. *My butt's in the sling now*, he thought, and looked up in time to see the unarmed Elder Thing reach out and pick him up. All the while piping a series of notes up and down the scale.

Mostyn tried struggling, but to no avail. The many tentacles held him firm. Jones rushed the creature and was quickly knocked to the floor. The three Elder Things departed with their prisoner.

————

The thought in Dotty's mind was a yell. *We have to do something!*

We will, my sister, came Helene's reply.

Dotty watched as Helene rematerialized just long enough to materialized her backpack inside the neck of one of the Elder Things guarding the rampway to the upper floor. The other creature dropped its weapon and tried to aid its companion, when it saw it choking. Helene, Dotty, and NicAskill appeared, and the creature vanished; only to have its star-shaped pseudo-foot appear in the floor, like some sort of decorative tile.

The first creature collapsed to the floor, tentacles clutching at its throat, and moments later stopped moving. Helene retrieved her backpack, and buried the alien in the floor next to its comrade.

Jones rushed to NicAskill, hugged her, and said, "Am I glad to see you!"

"There is no time, DC," Helene said. "We must rescue Mostyn Pierce." Helene, NicAskill, and Jones disappeared.

"Damn," Dotty said. "Helene, don't leave me here."

However, only silence met Dotty's command.

25

MOSTYN WASN'T TAKEN FAR. Just three doors down from where he and his team were being kept prisoner. In their dematerialized state, Helene, Jones, and NicAskill followed the aliens, after first taking the disruptors from the two dead aliens.

They watched the large plant and animal hybrids shepherd Mostyn into the building, after which they passed through the walls and took a position in a corner of the large room in which they found themselves.

Inside were a dozen of the Elder Things and twice that number of shoggoths. The latter lined one wall and looked like giant black exercise balls. No sound came from them, nor was there any movement.

Mostyn was left standing in the center of the room. The Elder Thing that had carried him in stood in front of him. Two others, armed with disruptors, stood on either side.

Jones looked at Helene and said in his mind, *I sure would like to know what's going on here.*

I think they are talking with Mostyn Pierce using their minds, Helene replied.

I thought they talked by means of that weird piping sound, NicAskill said.

Doesn't matter how they talk, Jones responded, *we need a plan to bust Mostyn out of here.*

Three against three dozen? NicAskill replied. *Good luck with that.*

———

A succession of pictures formed in Mostyn's mind, which he eventually understood as a question. They wanted to know how he and his people had reached the city. He formed a picture in his mind of a man with a shovel digging.

Let them figure that one out, he thought to himself.

Pictures of the destruction of the Russian base flashed through Mostyn's mind. He thought of a grassy field and a picnic.

This exchange went on for some time. The Elder Thing obviously wanting information, and Mostyn replying with pictorial versions of name, rank, and serial number.

What Mostyn would have liked was an understanding of their body language. Was he frustrating the thing? Getting it pissed off? Or were they immune to such emotions? And how, if he got out of this, could they capture one for Bardon so the human race could find out?

Pictures formed in his mind that Mostyn understood were meant to convey the idea that the Elder Things had created humans and that he was to worship them. Mostyn sent back a picture of himself defecating on an Elder Thing.

The response was what Mostyn thought to be an agitated piping over a considerable tonal range. In answer to the piping one of the shoggoths became animated. It rolled over to Mostyn and replaced the Elder Thing on Mostyn's left.

A brief series of notes came from the Elder Thing, and the shoggoth wrapped itself around Mostyn as an amoeba around a piece of food.

Helene, Jones, and NicAskill materialized, and a second later Jones and NicAskill opened fire. The armed Elder Thing on Mostyn's right disintegrated in a disruptor beam.

The alien that had been standing before Mostyn vanished. There was a cacophony of piping and the shoggoths came alive. Jones and NicAskill blasted two more of the odious entities into clouds of molecular dust, before they too were enveloped by the shoggoths just as Mostyn had been.

Helene dematerialized. However, she instantly rematerialized and found herself inside a translucent black, foul-smelling, sphere. She tried to dematerialize and found she could not. She was a prisoner. Inside a shoggoth.

26

MOSTYN GRADUALLY REGAINED CONSCIOUSNESS. He sat up and saw Jones and NicAskill were with him. But where were they? Wherever it was, the fetid smell was just about overpowering.

He scooched over and felt their pulses. They were alive. He turned his attention to the walls. They were an iridescent black, the iridescence providing a dim light. He reached out and touched the wall. It felt viscous, almost slimy. He pushed and there was give.

"We must be inside one of these damn shoggoths," he muttered.

He nudged Jones. "Come on, Jones. Sleepy time is over." He slapped his face. "Jones, get up. We have work to do." He slapped him again and Jones's eyes fluttered open.

"Wh-what happened?"

"Don't know, Jones."

"Where are we?"

"I think we're inside a shoggoth."

Jones sat up. "What?"

"I think we're imprisoned inside a living jail cell."

"How the hell are we going to get out? God, does it ever stink."

"Don't know. And if we're all together, then the things must have merged. How'd you get here?"

"Ms. Stealth."

"Where is Helene?"

"Don't know, Boss. Nicky and I blasted a couple shoggoths, then I found myself inside a bunch of goo, couldn't breathe, and that's the last I remember."

NicAskill groaned. "Where am I?"

"The boss thinks we're imprisoned inside a shoggoth."

NicAskill sat up. "Are you for real? God, what's that smell?"

"I don't know for sure," Mostyn said, "but that's my guess. It would certainly account for the smell."

"Now what do we do?" NicAskill asked.

Jones shrugged. "They took the blasters, so we're on our own."

"We get creative," Mostyn replied. "What do we have for weapons?"

They went through their pockets, the pouches on their belts, and what was attached to their belts that had escaped the eyes of the Elder Things.

"If it wasn't for Dotty giving me some goodies before I got whisked off to this place, we'd be in a world of hurt."

They had four handguns, three knives, two plastic-cased lye and aluminum grenades, four thermite grenades, several small boxes of waterproof matches, a couple lighters, their belts, and their creativity.

"Anyone have any paper?" Mostyn asked.

"I do," NicAskill said, and produced a couple packs of toilet paper and one of tissues.

"That's a start," Mostyn said. "Before we resort to more drastic means, let's see if we can cut our way out."

"Sounds good to me," Jones replied.

They each took a knife and began digging into the shoggoth.

————

"Listen up, people," Dotty began, but before she could continue she was interrupted by Julia Pridmore.

"Who put you in charge?" Pridmore said.

"I did," Dotty replied, "because I have the weapons." She pointed to the pile where the grenade launcher, sonic disruptor, the "shoggoth killer," and the other items Helene and NicAskill had left them.

"But you aren't Special Forces," Amber Bailey said.

Dotty looked at the young woman. "How long have you been with the OUP?"

"Two years," Bailey said.

"I have you beat four times over," Dotty replied. "Now listen up. Helene did us a favor by getting rid of the guards. We need to decide if we go out the back or the front."

Baker walked over to Dotty and stood next to her. He wanted his team to know, without saying anything, where he stood as to who he was going to follow.

Dotty smiled and nodded her thanks. "Any preference? Front or back?" she asked.

"We could check out the upper level and see if we can escape that way," Bailey said.

"Good idea," Dotty replied. "Go ahead."

Bailey picked up the E-753. "Doctor Smithson, would you care to join me?"

"Sure." He picked up a pistol from the pile of equipment and followed Bailey up the stairs.

Dotty picked up the sonic disruptor and handed it to Baker. "Merry Christmas. Do you think you can manage that?"

"Probably not. Something a little smaller maybe."

Dotty handed the sonic disrupter off to Doctor Dyer and gave Baker a pistol.

She gave the grenade launcher to Doctor Heidegger. "Julia, Fritz, you two take your pick of what's left here."

"This is wrong," Julia Pridmore said. There was a crazed and feverish look in her eyes. "We're the invaders. We don't belong here."

"Julia, none of that matters," Dotty said. "We need to get our people and get the hell out of here."

"I'm not killing any of these beings." Pridmore grabbed a pistol from the cache of weapons and equipment, racked the slide, and pointed it at Dotty. "And you aren't killing any of them either."

27

DOTTY LOOKED at the pistol in Pridmore's shaky hand. "Okay, Julia, we won't harm the Elder Things. How do you propose we get out of here?"

"We invaded their world," Pridmore replied. "Maybe we deserve whatever fate we get. Now put your gun down, Doctor Kemper."

"Okay, okay." Dotty squatted down, with her arms out wide, and set her pistol on the floor. She watched Doctor Pridmore's face and eyes and picked up movement behind Pridmore. Dotty slowly stood and watched Pridmore's shaky hand follow her.

Baker was standing on Dotty's left. No one was on her right. Dotty dropped, rolled to her right, and came up on her feet, while Heidegger delivered a punch to Pridmore's kidney.

The pistol discharged. The bullet ricocheting off the floor, and then the wall, narrowly missing Obermann.

Pridmore sank to the floor, dropping the pistol, and

Heidegger shoved her all the way down and sat on her.

Looking at Dotty, he asked, "What are we going to do with her?"

Before Dotty could answer, the door at the front of the building opened. Dotty snatched up her pistol and fired three rounds into the Elder Thing's head. It staggered back into the other alien that had been posted at the front door.

From the back came the other guards. Dyer pulled the trigger on the sonic disruptor, and the creatures were reduced to molecular dust.

Bailey and Smithson came down the stairs, as the remaining guard came through the front door. Bailey pulled the trigger on the "shoggoth killer" and nothing happened.

Heidegger stood up, grabbing Pridmore's pistol as he did so, and sent four rounds into the creature before it could fire its disruptor.

"Grab their weapons, get our equipment, and let's get the hell out of here," Dotty yelled. To Bailey, she said, "Leave that thing. Worthless R and D idiots."

"What about Pridmore?" Terri Lynn Dyer asked.

Doctor Pridmore sat up, and Dotty delivered a kick to the side of her head. Pridmore's eyes rolled up, and she fell over onto the floor.

"Leave her," Dotty said. "She's a liability and will get us killed."

"But she's one of us," Dyer protested.

"Not anymore," Dotty replied. "She gave up Mostyn and wants to give us up."

"But—"

Dotty pointed her pistol in Dyer's face. "No 'buts'. Let's go!"

"Okay. But I'm going to take her recorder."

"Do that," Dotty said, and headed for the back door, with the team following her.

"Where are we going?" Baker asked.

"To rescue our teammates, and then get the hell out of here," Dotty replied.

The street behind the building was narrower than the one in front, but still made for a fairly wide city street.

"How do we know where Mostyn and the others were taken?" Smithson asked.

"We don't," Dotty replied. "However, I saw them turn in this direction. So that's why we're going west and not east."

Dotty stopped at the door to the building next to the one in which they'd been held prisoner. She motioned for Bailey and Dyer to check it out, and told them to whistle if they came across anything.

"When you're done," Dotty said, "join us. We'll be in the building next door."

Bailey gave her a thumbs up, and she and Dyer went through the doorway.

Dotty and the rest of the team moved on to the next building. Just before entering, they heard "Tekeli-li! Tekeli-li!" being uttered behind them.

28

DIGGING into the protoplasmic substance that constituted the "flesh" of a shoggoth, Mostyn, Jones, and NicAskill got nowhere. At first the shoggoth just made that part of its body thicker. When they continued, the shoggoth began filling in the hollow cavity where they were imprisoned. Mostyn gave the order to stop before the creature had completely immobilized them.

"Okay," Mostyn said, "digging our way out isn't going to work. Let's try something a bit more drastic."

He took out a spare pistol cartridge, pried out the bullet, and emptied the powder into the toilet paper. When Jones realized what Mostyn was doing, a smile spread across his face, and he joined in.

"Oh, you're making an incendiary device," NicAskill said, and followed suit.

When the powder from nine cartridges had been emptied into the paper, Mostyn told them that was enough, and they'd give it a try.

"Jones, you make a hole. I'll shove the paper in, and, NicAskill, you light the paper. Jones, on three."

Mostyn counted, and when he reached three, Jones shoved his knife into the protoplasm and, using knife and fingers, created an opening. Mostyn shoved in the paper roll, and as Jones withdrew fingers and knife, NicAskill lit the paper with a match.

There was a brilliant flash, a string of high-pitched tones, a brief opening in the protoplasmic wall, then Mostyn, Jones, and NicAskill found themselves being surrounded by protoplasmic goo the color of midnight.

———

At the sound of "Tekeli-li," Dotty and the others with her turned to look in the direction from which it came.

"Holy shit," Bailey said. "There have to be hundreds of them!"

"Everybody inside!" Kemper shouted. "Quick!"

Five people piled through the doorway seconds ahead of the first wave of shoggoths, which ignored them and raced on down the street to the west.

Dotty looked around, found one of the circular ramps that passed for stairs, and indicated the team should ascend.

They ran up to the tenth floor and then out onto the roof. In the air were scores of flying Elder Things firing their disruptors into the mass of shoggoths on the ground that were locked in combat with shoggoths apparently controlled by the Elder Things.

Dotty took a small pair of binoculars out of a pouch and began sweeping the area around the building they were on.

"If you're trying to find Mostyn, I hope you're rubbing your rabbit's foot," Baker said.

"Say something positive, or don't say anything at all," Dotty shot back.

"We need to deal with what is, not what we want things to be," Baker replied.

The hand holding the binoculars dropped to her side, as Dotty turned and faced Baker. "If you don't shut up, I'm going to deck you, and leave you here for shoggoth food. Understood?"

"Sure, Dot." Baker, his free hand up, backed away.

Dotty went back to scanning the ground below.

————

Mostyn couldn't move and he couldn't breathe. He was completely encased inside the shoggoth. Like a food vacuole in an amoeba. In a matter of moments, he would black out and suffocate to death. This was it. He'd end up as shoggoth shit. Inside his head, he laughed.

Images flashed before his mind's eye. Dotty, Helene, Bardon, his parents, his siblings, Jones. That puzzled him. Of all people, why Jones?

He looked around. He was near the ceiling, looking down on the shoggoth. A series of piping sounds running up and down a wide tonal scale reached his ears. The shoggoth contracted, expanded, and rolled away.

A cough exploded from his mouth and he tried to catch

his breath. He rolled over. The stone floor was bitterly cold; even through his parka he felt the cold. Others were coughing and gasping for breath. Mostyn opened his eyes and looked around the room. It was empty, save for Jones, NicAskill, and Helene.

He got to his feet and staggered over to Helene. He knelt down next to her, felt for her pulse and finding one, shook her. "Helene! Wake up!"

He sent his thoughts to her. *Wake up! We have to leave!*

Helene's eyes fluttered open and in his mind he heard her voice. *I am here, Mostyn Pierce, my husband.*

He helped her to her feet and together they joined Jones and NicAskill.

"Where did everyone go?"

"That's the million dollar question, Jones," Mostyn replied.

"Who cares?" NicAskill said. "Let's get the hell out of here while the getting is good."

Mostyn went to the door and opened it. Pandemonium greeted his eyes. He saw an Elder Thing blast a shoggoth into atomic dust. He saw one shoggoth devour another, only to be devoured in turn.

"Weapons ready," Mostyn said. "It's a war zone out there. Follow me."

Out the door they went. A shoggoth bearing down on them vaporized before their eyes. Another came rolling towards them and it vanished.

"Back inside the building," Mostyn yelled.

They retreated and once inside, NicAskill said, "Maybe we can roof hop our way back."

Mostyn nodded. "Worth a try."

Helene held up her hand. "I sent my thoughts to my sister. She is nearby. We will go to her and the rest of the team."

In the blink of an eye, Mostyn, Jones, NicAskill, and Helene vanished.

29

MOSTYN, Jones, NicAskill, and Helene rematerialized on the rooftop where Dotty and the remaining team members had taken temporary refuge. Bailey and Dyer having rejoined their companions.

Mostyn took a headcount and asked where Doctor Pridmore was.

"She cracked up under the pressure," Dotty said. "Pulled a gun on me and was going to turn us over to the Elder Things. We subdued her, knocked her out, and left her behind."

The look on Mostyn's face was not a happy one.

"She truly lost it, Agent Mostyn," Doctor Obermann said. "Doctor Kemper did what she thought was best, and in the circumstances I had to agree with her."

"Shoggoth!" Jones yelled.

Before anyone could react, an Elder Thing hovering some fifty feet above them blasted the protoplasmic monstrosity into atoms. The alien aimed its weapon at Mostyn, dodged a long pseudo-tentacle, and flew off.

Bailey pressed the trigger of the captured alien disruptor and severed the "tentacle". It fell onto the rooftop with a sickly wet-sounding slap and rolled itself into a ball. Bailey fired the disruptor again, and the ball vaporized into a cloud of atomic dust.

"Let's get out of here," Mostyn ordered. "Back into the building."

The team members ran to the entrance and back down the circular ramp to the ground floor.

"Dotty, which way to where you left Pridmore?" Mostyn asked.

"Are you serious? She sold us down the river."

"Which way, Dot?"

Dotty Kemper glared at Mostyn and then gave it up. "It's a couple doors down."

"Okay, people, let's go."

The street was a chaotic mix of shoggoths and Elder Things locked in mortal combat. The pandemonium of a war zone. Elder Things in the air and on the ground blasting shoggoths. Shoggoths were battling shoggoths. And shoggoths were ripping the heads off of all the Elder Things they could find.

The humans, hugging the building walls, quickly moved back to the building they'd all left not that long ago.

"Is this where you left Doctor Pridmore?" Mostyn asked.

Dotty told him it was.

Mostyn pointed. "Jones, NicAskill, check the front. See if she's there."

Mostyn poked his head back out the door. A shoggoth stretched a pseudo-tentacle in his direction, and another shoggoth barreled into the creature. Mostyn swore and ducked back inside.

The high-pitched piping of 'Tekeli-li!" was everywhere and so were the flute-like sounds that ran up and down a very wide tonal scale.

Jones and NicAskill returned. "No sign of Doc Pridmore," Jones said.

Mostyn nodded, looked at his watch, and said, "We have an hour, maybe two of light left. We need to get back to the Vanesco and back to the surface. It is imperative we get what we've seen back to Bardon."

"How are we going to get there, Boss?" Jones asked. "We're in the middle of a war."

Mostyn smiled. "We're going to do the logical thing, Jones, and run like hell."

———

Down the street, Jones and NicAskill were checking out a building. Mostyn waited for the signal letting him know it was safe to send the rest of the team.

When it came, Mostyn sent his team on ahead, he and Bailey protecting the rear from any surprise attacks. When the team had made the run to Jones and NicAskill without a problem, Mostyn and Bailey followed.

They continued the caterpillar-like advance for eight

blocks. At that point Mostyn felt they were out of the main battle zone.

"Jones, NicAskill, you're the rear guard. Bailey, I want you in the middle. Now everyone follow me and run like a shoggoth is on your ass!"

Mostyn took off running, his team following him. The streets were empty. There was nothing to indicate any fighting had taken place in the area.

Then again, Mostyn thought, disruptors don't leave any evidence.

He tried raising Wulfe, who was with the Vanesco, on the radio to let him know they were coming. All he got in reply was static. However, Mostyn kept at it. He wanted to make sure the ice melting and boring machine was ready to high-tail it back to the surface.

Up ahead, Mostyn could see the space where the glacier had scraped the ground clean of the buildings the Elder Things had created, and beyond that the ruin of the city ramparts.

We just might make it, he thought.

From somewhere behind them sounded a chorus, and the word that was repeated over and over was "Tekeli-li!"

30

JONES AND NICASKILL turned and opened fire with the disruptors on the swarm of shoggoths rolling towards them. Mostyn told Bailey to get the rest of the team over the rampart and to the Vanesco. With Bailey seeing to the team's escape, Mostyn joined Jones and NicAskill, hoping to slow down the giant amoeboid monstrosities.

One of the iridescent black spheres bounced into the air, and, as it was coming down, Mostyn shot it with the sonic disruptor. It vanished, leaving a cloud of atom-sized dust.

Several more bounced into the air. Jones and Mostyn each blasted a creature, however two landed behind them. They cried, "Tekeli-li!", and vanished, revealing Dotty, holding an alien disruptor, and Helene.

"You two are supposed to be with the others," Mostyn said. The tone of his voice clearly revealing his displeasure.

"You're not dying without me," Dotty replied.

"We could use some help here," Jones yelled, pressing the bar that served for the trigger on the alien weapon.

Five shoggoths bounced into the air. NicAskill took out one before it got too far. Mostyn and Dotty took out two more directly overhead. Two, however, made it through, landing behind them.

A pseudo-tentacle shot out and wrapped itself around Helene, who vanished. Mostyn turned his weapon on the creature, but nothing happened. He dropped the disruptor, grabbed a plastic-cased lye and aluminum grenade, and hurled it at the monster. The grenade landed at the base of the shoggoth and exploded, enveloping the thing in a sheet of flaming hydrogen. Helene reappeared at Mostyn's side.

Another pseudo-tentacle grabbed Dotty. She turned the disruptor on it and the creature was turned into a dust cloud.

"Fall back!" Mostyn yelled.

NicAskill's weapon stopped firing. She hurled a thermite grenade at the monsters. Annihilating shoggoths in a conflagration of flames, and intense heat.

However, two of the hideous monstrosities survived and were rolling at high speed towards Jones and NicAskill. Jones aimed and pressed the trigger bar. Nothing happened. He spat out an expletive, threw the weapon at the creatures, and took off running, with NicAskill by his side.

Up ahead was the ruined rampart. Mostyn scanned it for an opening. But saw none. He saw Bailey helping Baker reach the top. Both waved upon seeing Mostyn and the others.

The continuously uttered, "Tekeli-li," was getting louder and louder as the shoggoths gained on their quarry.

High in the sky, Mostyn saw two Elder Things.

"Helene!" Mostyn yelled and pointed to the two aliens. "Tell them we need help."

Jones threw his last grenade at the creatures. They flattened to the ground, and it flew over them, exploding harmlessly behind the monsters.

Up above, one of the Elder Things swooped down and first one shoggoth and then the second vanished, leaving behind clouds of atomic dust that slowly drifted to earth. Then both of the hideous-looking aliens landed in front of Mostyn and his group.

The two faced Helene for about a quarter of a minute and then took off, returning to the air.

"We can go, Mostyn Pierce," she said. "They will protect us from the shoggoths until we are over the rampart."

"Move it, people! Let's get out of here!" Mostyn ordered.

The remaining members of Mostyn's team ran to the broken rampart and began the arduous climb over the smashed stones and masonry.

The Elder Things circled above and, on the ground, Mostyn and Jones kept an eye out for trouble.

When NicAskill, Kemper, and Helene had reached the top and begun their descent down the other side, Jones said, "Okay, Boss, head on up. I have your six."

"We'll go together, Jones. Come on."

The two agents climbed the mound of broken stone

blocks, and when they reached the top, they took hold of the descending lines and began their descent.

Halfway down, Mostyn slipped on a patch of ice, stumbled, and banged his left shin against the rock.

Jones signaled for help and Bailey climbed up. Together they got Mostyn down to the ground.

Dotty checked his leg. After a minute she said, "It's not obviously broken. Might just be bruised. Can you stand on it?"

Mostyn, gritting his teeth, tried to stand, and would've toppled over had Jones not caught him.

"I got you, Boss," Jones said, and began singing the song "Lean on Me."

Mostyn looked at him and said, "You don't look or sound like Bill Withers."

"Okay, okay," Jones replied. "Lean on me anyway."

"I have a simpler way, DC," Helene said, and with that she and Mostyn vanished.

Jones shook his head, and said, "C'mon, people, we have a bus to catch. Let's get moving."

The team set off for the Vanesco, Jones quietly humming "Lean on Me."

In the dematerialized state, Mostyn had no trouble moving. He watched his team begin the march to their transportation. Satisfied Jones had everything under control, he looked up and searched the sky. The Elder Things were gone.

31

MOSTYN AND HELENE rematerialized next to the Vanesco, or more properly what was left of it. The machine had been crushed as though it was made of cardboard. Frozen slime covered the machine, and Wulfe's decapitated body.

"I do not think this machine will work, Mostyn Pierce," Helene said.

Mostyn nodded. "I'd say your statement is true, as true can be."

He knelt down next to Wulfe's slimed and mutilated body, and winced as he did so. While still painful, the rematerializing seemed to have helped his shin.

"I'm sorry, Carl. We aren't going to be able to take you back with us," he said softly. "You or Jackson or Tamsworth or Schwartz or Pridmore."

Mostyn felt bad about that. All they would get was a memorial service. Their frozen bodies would lie in this place, perhaps forever. He stood. All except for Pridmore. If she was still alive, he hoped the Elder Things would take care of her. No guarantee of that, though. After all, as near as anyone knew, the Elder Things were as interested in their creations as a mother turtle is in her eggs. Although the odd behavior of the aliens regarding his own team, might give the lie to that general understanding.

The rest of the team arrived. When Jones saw Wulfe, he uttered the word, "Bummer," and turned away.

Obermann simply stood looking at the body of his assistant. His face was unreadable. He said nothing.

"I'm sorry for your loss, Doctor Obermann," Mostyn said.

The scientist and inventor looked at Mostyn and nodded. After a moment, he added, "A tragic waste of life."

"It is, indeed," Mostyn replied. To the rest of his team, he said, "Listen up, people. With no wheels, we're going to have to walk. In addition, we are going to be in the dark soon. Keep your flashlights and lamps ready. Before we set out for the mountains and our other machine, I need a weapons inventory."

He took note as each team member listed what he or she had remaining for weapons. When finished, Mostyn pursed his lips in thought. After a few seconds, he said, "Looks like we're in good shape with pistols and ammunition. We're down to our sonic disruptor and grenade launcher. We have a couple dozen grenades left, and we'll have to make do with that. Any questions?"

"When are we hiking out of here?" Dotty asked. "Walking's bad enough with the light. I don't want to walk over this terrain in the dark."

"If there are no more questions, we're leaving now."

A murmur rippled through the team indicating there were none.

"Very good," Mostyn said, "let's move out."

———

It was as though someone had flicked a light switch off. The world beneath the ice went from light to dark. Flashlights and wrist and helmet lamps were turned on. Little pools of blue-white light danced in the Stygian darkness.

Dotty tripped on a rock, cursed, and was saved from a fall by Smithson, who grabbed her arm just in time.

Doctors Dyer and Heidegger complained of the cold and their exhaustion. When Doctor Smithson tried to give them moral support, he was summarily told by Dyer to go copulate with himself.

Jones started singing the Springsteen hit "Dancing in the Dark." Mostyn chuckled. Other than the "dancing in the dark" line, he wasn't sure the lyrics were appropriate, but then the melody was upbeat and that's what his team needed.

Soon NicAskill joined in, followed by Baker. And Mostyn noticed something of a lift in the team's morale.

They crossed the empty riverbed and began the gradual climb to the foothills of the Gamburtsev Mountains, the beacon lights Jones had placed winking faintly in the inky blackness.

Mostyn dropped back, checking with each team

member. What he got from everyone was the same message. Cold. Hungry. Tired. Drained.

"Listen up, people. So no one gets lost, I want everyone to pair up. And since we have an odd number, I'll be the odd man out. Following me, I want Dubreuil and Kemper. Following them, I want Dyer and Heidegger. Next, Jones and Baker. Next, Obermann and Smithson. NicAskill and Bailey, you two will form the rear guard. Let's take five."

Dotty had managed to save one of the heaters, and everyone huddled around it the best they could in an attempt to warm hands and feet.

When the break was over, Mostyn made sure everyone was paired with his or her partner and in marching order. Then the trek to the Gamburtsevs, the Mountains of Madness, continued.

In the distance there were flashes of light, which Mostyn attributed to the disruptors of the Elder Things, and the faint but thinning chorus of "Tekeli-li! Tekeli-li!"

32

THE TREK back to the mountains and to the inner chambers that would take Mostyn and his people to the Vanesco was long and arduous. Lamp and flashlight beams were swallowed up by the Stygian inkiness of the eternal night that existed beneath the dome of glacial ice.

Mostyn pressed his team forward. A twenty-first century Shackleton encouraging his people to push on, to not give up, and to get back to the upper world that was their home.

"Just remember," he told them, "Heroism is nothing more than enduring for one more moment; and you all want to be heroes, don't you?"

Dotty muttered something under her breath. Mostyn didn't hear it, but had a good idea as to what she'd probably said.

The older members of the team were the hardest pressed. Heidegger, Obermann, and Baker found it increasingly difficult to keep up with the rest of the group, their partners taking on greater and greater responsibility to keep the three men moving.

When they reached the entrance to the system of tunnels and domiciles that honeycombed the mountain chain, Mostyn called a halt.

"Let's take fifteen. Drink some water. Have a bite of food. Share with those who don't have any."

Once again, Dotty set up the little heater.

Mostyn spoke with Helene and asked her if it would be possible for her to dematerialize the older men and get them to the vehicle.

"I can do that, Mostyn Pierce," she answered him.

"Good. Go ahead. The rest of us will meet you there as soon as we can."

She kissed him, rounded up the three men, and all four vanished.

Mostyn then announced to the remaining members of his team that Helene was taking the older men, in a dematerialized state, back to the remaining Vanesco, which would allow the rest of them to make better time.

"That climb is going to be a bitch, Mostyn," Dotty said. "No matter who's climbing it. There are miles of tunnels in there."

Mostyn nodded. "I hear you, Dot. We here, though, are in better shape to tackle them."

Dotty snorted her displeasure, but said nothing.

"Okay folks, break's—"

Mostyn abruptly stopped speaking, and everyone heard it. Somewhere in the pitch black eternal night came a commingled piping over a wide tonal range and the endlessly repeated word, "Tekeli-li!"

———

Mostyn wasted no time getting his people together and the team fled into the mountain's tunnel system. He put Jones and Bailey in the rear of the formation. Jones had the sonic disruptor, and Bailey the grenade launcher.

The team walked briskly back the way they came; retracing their steps to Obermann's ice boring and melting machine, which was their ticket home.

The piping and that hideous word were gradually getting closer. Even in the tunnel, Mostyn could hear it. This did not bode well for the remaining members of his team. He was, though, out of options. Now it was down to which of the two could move faster: the humans or the shoggoths. And everyone knew the answer. It wasn't the humans.

Through the tunnels they trotted, trying to put as much distance as possible between themselves and the hideous creatures whose very existence was a blasphemy of science.

There was a change in the piping and in that noxious word. The sound was at once confined and yet echoed through the tunnels, reverberating through the air and through stone. The shoggoths were now in the tunnel system.

Were these the survivors of the battle with the Elder Things? Or were these creatures a group that had sniffed out the human presence and gone forth to search and destroy?

Mostyn didn't care. It didn't matter. Either scenario meant their death if the monsters caught up with them. It was as simple as that.

Bailey yelled, "Grenade!"

Mostyn was barely able to reach the stone floor when the thermite grenade detonated. For less than a minute the heat in the tunnel was intense and the passage brightly illuminated by the burning shoggoths. Then once again the darkness and cold returned.

Trying to take cover, Doctor Dyer stumbled and twisted her ankle. Mostyn switched places with Jones so he could help her walk.

The tunnel was momentarily quiet. Mostyn waved his arm, signaling his team members to press on.

And then there it was, the piping running up and down a wide tonal scale, and that word. That goddamn word, "Tekeli-li! Tekeli-li!," repeated over and over again.

33

MOSTYN AND BAILEY waited until the team was a couple hundred yards ahead of them before they started jogging after them.

The sound of the shoggoths was getting closer and closer. Mostyn and Bailey broke into a run. He radioed ahead to Jones and told him they needed to double time.

Around the curve in the tunnel, some two hundred feet behind them, rolled the first of the black iridescent nightmares. In their headlamps it looked as though it were a gargantuan spheroid made of opal. Eyes and mouths appearing and disappearing on the opaline plasma.

Bailey turned and fired a lye and aluminum grenade on the run. The bomb flew down the tunnel, bounced off the wall, and exploded mid-air behind the lead creature, which was engulfed in the flames of the hydrogen explosion and turned into a cinder.

There was only a momentary lull in the ghastly refrain, before it started up again.

"How many of those things are there?" Mostyn muttered.

Bailey panted, "Wish I knew, sir."

"Rhetorical question," Mostyn replied, as he turned his head to look at their pursuers.

More of the repellently foul things rolled around the curve in the tunnel.

"There's at least four of those things back there," Mostyn said, as he turned, stopped, fired the disruptor, saw one vanish, and turned again, continuing his run up the tunnel.

A loathsome stench began to reach Mostyn's nose, which meant only one thing: the odious fiends were gaining on them.

"I'm down to four grenades," Bailey said, while holding the grenade launcher over her shoulder and pulling the trigger.

There was a sound like that of a rifle firing. The grenade skipped off the tunnel floor and exploded in the midst of the shoggoths. The Bardonite grenade showered the alien obscenities with burning and dissolving agents. The sounds the creatures made, even to human ears, indicated intense agony and they melted away into puddles of protoplastic goo.

Mostyn looked down the tunnel. His head and wrist lamps picked up an opalescent nightmare rolling toward them, screaming, "Tekeli-li!"

He shouldered the sonic disruptor, aimed, and pulled the trigger. Nothing happened.

"What the hell?"

"It must be discharged," Bailey said. She fired the grenade launcher, dropping a thermite grenade in front of the creature. The little bomb exploded, incinerating the monstrosity. "Let's go, sir."

Mostyn dropped the weapon, and he and Bailey ran up the tunnel.

On once again hearing that damnable word, he looked back on saw a lone opalescent sphere, eyes and mouths appearing and disappearing, steadily gaining on them.

He radioed to Jones. "We have a shoggoth on our butt and the disruptor is dead. Can you set up an ambush?"

"There's a cross tunnel up ahead," Jones replied. "I think we can set one up there, Boss."

"Do it."

"On it."

"We aren't going to make it, sir," Bailey said. "Jones and the others are seven, eight hundred feet ahead of us."

Mostyn knew Bailey was right. The shoggoth would be on them before they ever got to where Jones was setting up the ambush. He was the team leader, and knew what he had to do. He had a thermite grenade. If he detonated the little incendiary device just before the abnormality engulfed him, he could destroy the thing.

The loathsome stench of the hideous monster was increasingly palpable, which meant it was getting closer and closer.

Mostyn, panting for breath, said, "Go on, Bailey. I'll stop this thing. Tell Dotty I love her."

Bailey replied by saying, "Sorry, sir," and shoved Mostyn.

He stumbled and fell in a heap, while Bailey stopped, took out her remaining two thermite grenades, pulled the pins, and ran towards the shoggoth.

Mostyn screamed an ear-splitting. "No!"

Just as the creature was about to engulf Bailey, Mostyn saw the safety levers fly away. Four seconds later, two brilliant yellow-white sheets of flame ripped through the black protoplasm of the monstrosity, illuminating the tunnel.

34

THE JUMBO JET was winging its way over the South Pacific, on its way to Honolulu, Hawaii, where it would refuel and take the remainder of Mostyn's team to the District of Columbia and home.

While at McMurdo, Mostyn had sent an initial report to Bardon, who had simply replied, "Good work." That was it. Mostyn couldn't figure out what was the good work they'd done. Gone were Parker Jackson, Amber Bailey, JoEllen Tamsworth, and Sandy Schwartz. Gone, too, Obermann's assistant, Carl Wulfe, and Doctor Julia Pridmore. Her fate was unknown, but she had to be presumed dead. And even if she wasn't, she'd not be leaving the city of the Elder Things anytime in this lifetime.

Helene was sitting on Mostyn's left, chatting away with Jones and NicAskill. Dotty sat on his right and was reading. Mostyn was deep in thought.

What had they actually accomplished? Was it worth the lives of six people? The most important discovery was that the Elder Things were still alive. They had not been completely exterminated by the shoggoths. The second most important discovery was that the aliens were at war with the renegade shoggoths over control of the sacred city.

But was that worth six lives? Mostyn wasn't convinced it was. But he wasn't Bardon and certainly didn't know what Bardon knew. Nevertheless, he would see in his mind's eye Bailey's self-immolation to destroy the shoggoth till death shut down his brain.

She had saved him, and the rest of the team. While he'd contemplated, she'd acted. He was getting too old for this. He had too much baggage and it slowed him down.

Special Agent in Charge Pierce Mostyn leaned his head back against the headrest and closed his eyes. God, was he ever tired. He pictured in his mind a house with a white picket fence in some Midwestern city's suburb. Deep in the heart of flyover country. Away from everything. And children. He'd like that. He never thought he'd think so; but, yes, children would be nice. A swing set in the backyard and a sandbox. Those would be mandatory.

He opened his eyes, cast a glance at Dotty, and then one towards Helene, and closed them again. A smile touched his lips. *Daddy,* he thought. *Yeah, I could get used to that.*

EPILOGUE

BARDON WAS HIS EBULLIENT SELF, puffing away on his bent bulldog, the sweet Virginia pipe tobacco scenting his office. On the other side of Bardon's desk sat Pierce Mostyn.

"A very valuable mission, Pierce, my boy, very valuable. You weren't able to capture an Elder Thing, but a very valuable mission nevertheless."

"How so, sir?" Mostyn couldn't get those six deaths out of his mind. Especially Bailey's.

"Because of the intel you gathered. We have photographs of the sacred city of the Elder Things. We have Doctor Pridmore's recorded notes. We know the Elder Things are alive and bent on taking back the city from the shoggoths. It also seems the Elder Things are not as degenerate as Dyer thought. And the fact there is a massive bubble in the glacial ice..." Bardon closed his eyes, his face positively beaming.

When he opened them, he looked at Mostyn. "I'm very

sorry for the people you lost. They will get the highest of honors and their families will be well compensated."

"Compensated with what, sir?" Mostyn stripped his voice of all emotion. He was angry, but didn't want to show his feelings to Bardon.

"The only thing we can compensate them with. Money."

"Rather poor compensation, that. Don't you think, sir?"

"That I do, Pierce. That I do."

There was a pause, and then Mostyn spoke. "Uh, sir, I've—"

"Where are you going on your time off?" Bardon asked, interrupting Mostyn.

"That's what I wanted to talk to you about, sir." Mostyn cleared his throat. "I've decided to retire, sir."

The air was still. Mostyn looked at his boss, and Bardon looked back at him. How long they sat there, Mostyn didn't know. It seemed like forever, although he realized it couldn't have been more than a few seconds.

Bardon sighed and leaned back in his chair. "What, pray tell, has made you come to this decision?"

"Bailey, sir. We both had the same thought, but I hesitated just a second too long. I think my feelings for Dotty and Helene got in the way of my duty. She outsmarted me and sacrificed herself for the team, when it should've been me."

"I see." Bardon set his pipe down. "Yes, her death was tragic. She was a good soldier. She did her duty. And you did yours. You have nothing to be ashamed of. So how can I get you to change your mind? You are my most valuable agent, Pierce. Your analytical ability is more important than any self-sacrificial valor. And I need that ability. I need it to stop them."

"Thank you, sir. I appreciate your confidence. But you can't change my mind." Mostyn pulled a folded sheet of paper from his suit coat pocket. "Here's my notice of retirement, effective immediately." He handed the paper to Bardon, who took it, looked it over, and set it on his desk.

"Very well, Pierce. I can't possibly express my sorrow at seeing you leave."

"Thank you, sir. That means a lot. My office is cleaned out." Mostyn stood and extended his hand. After a moment, Bardon stood and shook hands with his now former agent.

"I wish you the best, Pierce."

"Thank you, sir."

Mostyn turned and left. When the door had closed, Bardon returned to his chair. He picked up the sheet of paper, read the brief statement again, and set it back down on his desk.

The director of the Office of Unidentified Phenomena closed his eyes and pursed his lips. His hands were flat on his desk. He remained that way for a minute or two. When he opened his eyes, a smile touched his lips.

He got up and went to his sideboard situated between the statues of Cthulhu and Shub-Niggurath. Prizes taken from the expedition to K'n-yan. He poured himself a glass of port. A very fine vintage port. He raised the glass to each of the deities and took a sip.

"I guess I have my work cut out for me." He turned and

looked at the door through which his best agent had recently passed. "However, as you well know, Pierce, my boy, no one ever truly leaves the OUP. No one."

Bardon raised his glass. "To your speedy return, my friend."

A WORD FROM CW

I hope you enjoyed *In the Shadow of the Mountains of Madness*.

If you did, please leave a review where you bought the book and on your favorite social media sites. Your review is like word of mouth advertising. And it is pure gold.

Enter my World

Enter my world. A world of terror on a cosmic scale. Just click, tap, or scan the QR code below.

Fear is the most primal of human emotions. And fear of the unknown is the most terrifying of all fears.

If you are new to the Pierce Mostyn Paranormal Investigations series, then *In the Shadow of the Mountains of Madness* is an excellent entry point into the series and into my world.

In addition to my Pierce Mostyn Paranormal Investigations books, I've written short stories set in the world of the macabre and arcane. Many of which are only available to folks on my mailing list.

So just click, tap, or scan the QR code to enter my world of terror and the macabre. You will get a free copy of *The Feeder* and you'll get my monthly email of news and curated contact. Terror awaits!

CONTINUE THE ADVENTURE!

The paranormal investigations of Pierce Mostyn will continue. Book 9 will be coming out in the new future. In the meantime, if you haven't read *Nightmare in Agate Bay*, the first book in the series, you might want to give it a read and get in on the action from the beginning.

Nightmare in Agate Bay. Where they're staging a comeback. And they want us out of the way.

There are rumors that an ancient evil has resurfaced in the decaying Lake Superior town of Agate Bay. Pierce Mostyn, special agent with the ultra-secret Office of Unidentified Phenomena, is tasked with finding out if the rumors are true. If they are, Mostyn must take appropriate action to contain or eliminate the threat.

When he and his team arrive in Agate Bay, they find a virtual ghost town. The few remaining inhabitants quickly show themselves to be hostile and threatening. And they appear to be suffering from some manner of strange disease. Or are they?

However when Mostyn and his team finally discover the truth, can they get out of town in time to save the world? Or will they too become part of the hideous nightmare in Agate Bay?

If you love weird fiction, horror, monsters, humor, thrilling action, and the Cthulhu Mythos, get in on Pierce Mostyn's adventure today — if you dare!

Nightmare in Agate Bay is available at your favorite online store. Click, tap, or scan the QR code and check it out!

BOOKS BY CW HAWES

CW is a multi-genre author.

The books below are portals to his many exciting worlds. And no AI was used in the writing of these books. Books by a human for a human.

Pierce Mostyn Paranormal Investigations

The X-Files meets Cthulhu. Pierce Mostyn does battle with inter-dimensional monsters bent on the destruction of humanity.

Nightmare in Agate Bay
Stairway to Hell
Terror in the Shadows
Van Dyne's Vampires
The Medusa Ritual
Demons in the Dunes
Van Dyne's Zuvembies

In the Shadow of the Mountains of Madness

Justinia Wright Private Investigator Mysteries

Justinia Wright is the PI with panache. These slow burn mysteries, written in homage to Rex Stout's Nero Wolfe, are sure to satisfy your craving for intriguing puzzles, quirky characters, and wise-cracking humor.

Vampire House and Other Early Cases of Justinia Wright, PI
Festival of Death
Trio in Death-Sharp Minor
But Jesus Never Wept
The Conspiracy Game
A Nest of Spies
When Friends Must Die
Death Makes a House Call
To Right a Wrong
The Nine Deadly Dolls
Ripples on the Pond
Christmas with the Wrights
Minneapolis's Finest
Jack in the Box
Sauerkraut Days
Justinia Wright Private Investigator Omnibus Edition

Magnolia Bluff Crime Chronicles

Tense slow burn mysteries set in our favorite town in the Texas Hill Country.

Death Wears a Crimson Hat

Ten Million Ways to Die
Who Mourns Elektra?
Death by Moonlight

The Rocheport Saga

A post-apocalyptic adventure series in the style of cozy catastrophes such as *Earth Abides* and *Day of the Triffids*. Join Bill Arthur as he strives to build a new and better world on the ashes of the old.

The Morning Star
The Shining City
The Divided City
The Troubled City
By Leaps and Bounds
Freedom's Freehold
Take to the Sky

Decopunk

Alternative history adventures in a world where World War II never happened and swing is still king.

From the Files of Lady Dru Drummond
The Moscow Affair
The Golden Fleece Affair

Rand Hart Adventures
Rand Hart and the Pajama Putsch

Tales of the Macabre

For the horror lover in you.
  Do One Thing For Me
  Metamorphosis
  What the Next Day Brings
  Ancient History

Anthologies

Enjoy CW's stories in these short story collections.
  The Phantom Games
  Beyond the Sea
  Overmorrow
  Arachnapocalypse! The Anthology
  Once Upon a WolfPack

Available at your favorite online retailer.

ABOUT CW HAWES

CW Hawes has written over 50 novels and shorter works of fiction. He was also an award-winning poet and had over 200 poems appear in ezines and and print.

He is a founding member of the Underground Authors and was the impetus for the highly successful Magnolia Bluff Crime Chronicles series.

After 35 years of working in county government, he retired at the beginning of 2015 and began a second career as a fictioneer. Perhaps some of the horrors Pierce Mostyn faces can be traced to his creator's own experiences in county government and beyond. Perhaps.

CW lives in Southern California. He enjoys reading, writing, chess and other board games, his daily morning walk, and contemplating the meaning of life while smoking his pipe. He also hasn't met a doughnut or a pizza he doesn't like, is something of a tea snob, and rocks out to Handel and Vaughan Williams.

You can get curated content and the occasional free story

when you join his mailing list, and you can reach him at his website, on X, and also Facebook.

To join his mailing list, click, tap, or scan the QR code:

To visit him on his website, click, tap, or scan the QR code:

To visit him on X, click, tap, or scan the QR code:

To visit him on Facebook, click, tap, or scan the QR code: